Flint

Book 1:

Choosing Sides . . .

Flint

Book 1:

Choosing Sides . . .

Treasure Hernandez

www.urbanbooks.net

Urban Books
1199 Straight Path
West Babylon, NY 11704

First Trade Paperback Printing February 2008
First Mass Market Paperback Printing December 2008
Printed in the United States of America

10   9   8   7   6   5   4   3

Submit Wholesale Orders to:
Kensington Publishing Corp.
C/O Penguin Group (USA) Inc.
Attention: Order Processing
405 Murray Hill Parkway
East Rutherford, NJ 07073-2316
Phone: 1-800-526-0275
Fax: 1-800-227-9604

ACKNOWLEDGMENTS

For and foremost, I'd like to thank God for the abundance of blessings He's bestowing me; It is with His love and guidance from which my peace flows.

I'd like to thank Carl Weber and my girl, Arvita Glenn, for this opportunity of a lifetime to follow my dreams. Shout outs to all my brothers and sisters on lockdown. Though things may seem bleak now, please believe the sun will soon shine, so hang in there, keep it real and keep it positive. I'm looking forward to coming out in two years, but until then, holla at a sister.

Treasure Hernandez
c/o Urban Books
1199 Straight Path
West Babylon, NY 11704

Love & peace,
Treasure

Chapter One

"There go your boy," Nikki whispered to Halleigh as they sat in the cafeteria watching Malek Johnson lope into the room.

Halleigh glanced up, and her thin, glossy lips were instantly graced with a smile at just the sight of him. Malek stood out like a Hollywood celebrity against the crowd of Flint Central High School students milling about the lunchroom. At six feet, five inches tall and well-built, it wasn't just his clean-cut, Sean John look, but he also had a charismatic presence that commanded nothing but the utmost respect. And he received it. He also had a smile that melted the panties off many females throughout the school, with the exception of Halleigh Walters.

Yeah, Mr. Malek might have looked good and all, draped in his blue, gray, and white plaid Sean Jean button-up and his midnight blue Sean John jeans, and any other girl would have been happy to stitch his name on her "Vickie" panties. But Halleigh, in her own gentle presence, demanded her own respect, and she couldn't get it by becoming just another shoestring hole in his Jordan's, to be laced up with all those other tricks he'd been with. She had to show that she was a different kind of breed and unlike those other hoodrats he'd fucked with before.

After realizing that she was smiling just like some of those other groupies that couldn't wait for him to pass them by just so they could get high off of his lingering scent, Halleigh quickly got rid of it and replaced it with the twisting up of her lips and a shrug of her shoulders. "Yeah, I see him," she said nonchalantly. She poked at the entrée that the school cook referred to as spaghetti, but from what she could see, it was just a bunch of noodles with a couple hunks of ground burger here and there. And the last time she checked, spaghetti had sauce.

Nikki told her, "Girl, all I can say is that you crazy. I would've been gave that nigga some, if I was you. You know he's going to the league. You need to be trying to have his baby. That NBA money will have you set for life."

As she spoke, Nikki watched Malek's every move. His popularity was evident. His confident swagger not only demanded Halleigh's and Nikki's attention, but everyone grinned and called out his name as he passed, like the act of saying his name alone made them part of his dream—the one to escape the ghetto. He was the number one high school basketball prospect in the state. In the world, for all they knew.

The students acted like paparazzi or would-be agents.

"Waddup? Malek, you the man."

"Malek, did you decide where you gon' go yet?"

"Malek, you gon' sign if you get drafted?"

Malek worked the crowd, slapping hands with some of his teammates that stood in his path; a path that one would think should have been laid out with a red carpet. He gave dap to other classmates and pounds to a few of his friends he'd grown up with. Without missing a beat, he bobbed his head to an invisible rhythm, as a five-person BET camera crew followed his every move.

Malek was expected to be the number one pick in the upcoming draft, and he was high from all the attention he had been receiving over the past couple of weeks. Malek hadn't decided if he would enter the league or if he would try his hand at college first, and the anticipation over his decision was killing sports fans all across the country. Malek was the man of the hour, and everybody wanted a piece of him. Even Halleigh wanted a piece of him, literally. She could just taste him, but would never dare to let that little fact be known.

"Shut up, Nikki," Halleigh snapped. "It's not like that with me and him. I'm not trying to trap anybody. I just like being around him."

"Just like being around him? Girl, you better do more than just be around that nigga. Hell, a fly buzzing around his head is just being around him.

You better give him some of that thing right there"— Nikki pointed to Halleigh's girlhood—"before the next chick steals on your man." Nikki looked around the cafeteria at the damn-near drooling chicks. "These scandalous bitches don't just see a good-looking brotha when they look at Malek. They see dollar signs. They practically begging him to fuck with them." Nikki was seriously trying to put her friend up on game. *Shit, I'd throw some pussy his way if I thought he would take it,* she thought to herself.

Nikki flipped her long hair out of the way before taking a bite of her roll that accompanied the spaghetti. Her dark brown locks were wavy now, after having worn her hair in French braids for the last week. Against her dark brown, smooth skin her hair made her look exotic, like she was from the islands or something. She was gorgeous. A chocolate delight, to say the least. Standing at average height, around five foot, six inches, Nikki was also of average size, a twelve in winter months and a ten in the summer months. She made it a point to shed any extra pounds she had accumulated in the winter months by the time the school year was up. She had to look good in a two-piece for whenever she went to the pool. All the ballers hung out at the pool, on the prowl for a summer bunny, which meant for some lucky female, three months of shopping, eating out, and as a bonus, maybe they'd even get a tennis bracelet. She had managed to earn two since her ninth grade year. And if her best friend played her cards right with Malek, she too could begin her collection. That's why she had to come to her from the hip, letting her know that if she didn't show her hand, another bitch might trump her ass.

"I'm not worried about the next girl," Halleigh said. "I know what me and Malek got. He ain't worried about nobody else but me. It's me and him against the world."

Halleigh was, in fact, as confident as she sounded. Ever since she first met Malek back in eighth grade, long before he became the high school basketball star that he was today, he had always been nothing but kind and respectful to her. Back then, they had shared a history class together when the two of them, along with two other students, were placed in a group to work on a project together. At the time, Malek was kicking it with some girl named Nessa, but his attraction to Halleigh was evident from the way he stared at her whenever she was discussing something about the project. Malek was fine, and no girl in her right mind wouldn't have had a mutual attraction. But what really drew Halleigh to him was the fact that he never came on to her. She assumed it was because he respected his relationship with Nessa.

After their history class together, Malek and Halleigh didn't really talk much, but whenever they passed each other in the halls, the unspoken attraction took up the space between them. Even after Malek and Nessa broke up, when other girls would swarm him, trying to be his next chick, Halleigh never pushed up on him. She figured if he wanted her, he'd come to her; she shouldn't have to chase after no man.

By the same token, with all the girls chasing after him, Malek felt that if Halleigh was interested in being his girl, then she would show her interest by doing the same thing the other girls were doing, but she didn't. So Malek did go on to kick it with plenty of other girls before finally, in eleventh grade, putting his pride aside and going after Halleigh and making her his one and only.

When they first got together all kinds of whispers and rumors made the rounds of the school. "Girl, he just gon' screw you and dump you like he did all them other girls."

"Don't get comfortable. He loves 'em and leaves 'em."

"If all the other chicks didn't have what it takes to keep him, what makes you think you do?"

"I hear he's sleeping with you and every other girl in the school."

And although, in most cases, the gossip might have gotten to other couples and put a dent in their relationship, it only made Halleigh and Malek more bound and determined to prove everybody wrong.

Halleigh never let the rumors that Malek was fucking so-and-so get to her. Some of the girls started the rumors themselves, just to try and break up the couple so that they could have dibs, but it never worked. And it never convinced Halleigh to give up her own virginity just so she could keep her man.

"Yeah, all that is cool, but you never gonna lose that cherry if you keep waiting for shit to happen. You have to make shit happen." Nikki eyeballed Halleigh with a knowing look.

"Yeah, whateva." Halleigh tossed her hair flippantly. Her hair wasn't as long as Nikki's, but it was a good length, to her shoulders. Halleigh always wore it flat-iron straight with feathered side bangs down her face. Light skinned and not as gorgeous as Nikki or as tall, she was still cute in the face. Cute enough to have Malek sniffing behind her for all those years, anyway. And she had a nice figure that was lean and toned, but meaty and thick in all the right places.

Somewhat peeved, Halleigh arose from the table and made her way over to Malek. Halleigh didn't care what Nikki said. She didn't see her with any steady boyfriend, so what did she know? All those drawers she had dropped, and where was her man? Doesn't matter how beautiful a girl is on the outside, if niggas know that everybody done been inside, they ain't trying to make her wifey. And although Halleigh loved Nikki like a stepsister, she was the prime example of why she hadn't given it up. She wanted to make sure that when she did have sex, it would be with someone who she knew loved her for her and not for what was between her legs. And last night, she had come to the conclusion of who that person was.

After making her way to Malek, Halleigh quickly took her place under one of his arms. He introduced her to the world as he gazed into the cameras. "This is my girl, Halleigh." He looked down at her and kissed her on the forehead. "This is my boo."

This time, Halleigh let the smile stay painted on her lips as she mouthed, "Hi" to the cameras and waved. Standing by Malek's side while he was being interviewed, she was so glad she'd worn her orange designer dress to school that day. She couldn't stop smiling if someone had paid her. Every time she was around him, she felt lucky to be a part of his life.

Standing there together in front of the cameras, they were in sharp contrast to one another. He was tall and slim; she was short and thick. He was a dark sienna brown, and she was a rich persimmon color. He was full of personality and animated, and she was laid-back and plain.

Even though Halleigh looked innocent, a lot of people thought that she was a freak behind doors, that usually it was the quiet ones that you had to look out for. So they figured Malek was probably only with her for what she could do for him behind closed doors. And a lot of people also thought that she was only with Malek because of his promising future, but she knew the deal. She was with him because she loved him. They had been dating since their junior year and were friends long before that, not to mention he knew her like no one else did.

Halleigh stood by him until the end of his interview, and then they strolled out of the cafeteria together. He kissed the top of her head as they made their way down the hallway. "So what's all that you were talking on the phone last night?" Malek asked. He couldn't wait for the opportunity to bring up that conversation today. He needed to make sure that his conversation last night with her wasn't just a dream, or that she hadn't been half-'sleep when she'd called him up late last night.

Halleigh blushed. She thought back to the conversation she'd had with him the night before. The phone call she'd made after coming to the conclusion that Malek really did love her for her and not just for the sex. Because she hadn't given him any. But now she wanted to. She knew deep down inside that she didn't have to have sex to keep him. She wanted to have sex with him because she loved him. So, before she could coward out and second-guess herself, after midnight she'd made this call telling him how much she loved him. And after he confirmed his love for her, something she already knew, she promised him that she would give him her virginity the night of the championship game, which was that night.

She'd held out for the entire two years that they had been dating and felt like it was time to take their relationship to the next level. They would be graduating soon. They would be adults and would no longer have to put up with all the childish he-said, she-said and rumors that high school life entailed. And although she hated to admit it, Halleigh was also beginning to take heed to Nikki's warnings.

Now that they would be leaving the high school life behind, there would be the real world. She'd be up against real women. She didn't want to give another girl room to take her place. She wanted Malek to be completely satisfied with her, mind and body. "Can I ask you a question?" she inquired right when the school bell rang.

Malek stopped walking, once the two stood at his locker. "You know you can ask me anything." He fumbled around with his lock, trying to put in his combination, but was unsuccessful.

Halleigh, who knew the combination, operated the lock for him and successfully unlocked it. While Malek opened up his locker and began shifting through it, she glimpsed around at the throngs of student flowing throughout the high school corridor. She made sure no one was within earshot then said, "I'm not saying that I don't want to, because I do." She inhaled a deep breath. "But . . . if we didn't have sex, if I never called you last night and told you that I would, you know . . . would you leave me?" Halleigh's face scrunched up and worry tinged her voice. "I mean, with all those college girls out there, or just women, period."

Malek looked down at her as she lowered her head and tried to avert his stare. He placed his finger on her lips to silence her. "Is that what you really think? I mean, is that what *you* think"—he gently poked her heart with his finger—"and not what somebody is putting in your ear?" Malek knew how other broads were, how they liked to get into other girls' ears who weren't out sexin' everybody like they were.

Halleigh didn't reply.

Malek, after getting everything he needed from

10

his locker, closed it and continued talking. "Hal, you don't have to do nothing you don't want to do."

"I know, I know, but I don't want none of these other chicks offering you something that I'm not giving you. Eventually, you will get what you want from someone else," she whispered, clutching her books to her chest. "It's not like you ain't gotten it before." She turned to walk toward her next class, her eyes watering from the very thought of Malek choosing another girl over her. None of that stuff had ever bothered her before, but now, all of a sudden, and now that life after high school was approaching, she couldn't shake off the thoughts as easily as before.

"It's not like that with us," Malek tried to assure her, as they walked side by side. "I thought I've shown you that by now. I'm not trying to fuck with nobody but you. These girls only chasing after me because they think I'm about to come into some money. I know where your head is at. I had to chase after you, remember?" he said in a playful manner. He lifted her chin while the two continued walking down the hall. "I'm gon' be with you always. I'm with you for you, the same way that you are with me for me. I know that if all the material shit that comes along with being a basketball star is gone tomorrow, you would still be here holding me down." Malek stopped walking. Then his tone became serious. "You the only one who really cares about me on the inside. Everyone else just wants to use me and get a piece of me."

Halleigh stood still next to her man, absorbing his every word.

"I love you, Halleigh, and I'll wait as long as you need me to. I'm not going to lie, I know you mentally and emotionally, but I'm trying to know you physically too. But, baby girl, I'll wait until you are comfortable. You're my world, you know that. At least, I thought you did."

Halleigh stared into her man's eyes, searching for congruency between what his eyes said and the words his mouth uttered. His eyes didn't crinkle teasingly like they did when he was joking with her. He was dead serious. It was more than just his eyes that told the truth. Halleigh could hear the sincerity behind his words, and in her heart, she knew that after the game that night, she would be in his bed. "I know, I know," she replied.

"So you gon' let me get up in that or what?" he whispered in her ear, pushing her hair behind her double-pierced ears that held the diamond studs he'd purchased for her as a birthday gift.

She hit him in the stomach and laughed.

"You know I'm just playing with you," he offered. Malek continued walking with Halleigh right by his side.

"Okay, let's make a bet," she proposed. "If you score over 40 points in the championship, then I got you guaranteed, if not, you just gon' have to wait a little bit longer."

Malek's eyes lit up. He liked the game she was playing. "How much longer?"

"Until graduation."

"That's four months away!" he exclaimed.

Just then, they stopped walking and stood in the doorway to Halleigh's next class.

"Then you better get off tonight if you don't want to wait," she said in a flirtatious and challenging tone. She smiled mischievously, hinting at their night of pleasure to come.

As Malek leaned over and kissed her lightly on the lips, Halleigh's teacher, Ms. Gulley, announced, "That's enough, Mr. Johnson," interrupting their intimate moment.

Halleigh laughed and pushed Malek, feinding not having anything to do with the kiss.

"Sorry, Ms. Gulley," Malek said, throwing two fingers in the air and winking at Halleigh before he strolled up the hallway.

"And pull up those pants!" Ms. Gulley bellowed. She smiled and shook her head. "Nobody wants to see your behind."

Speak for yourself. Halleigh smiled then turned and headed into the classroom.

"Malek Johnson is having one of the best ball games of his life, ladies and gentlemen," the ESPN sports commentator said as he watched the game in awe. "This is amazing. It is only the third quarter and he already has 32 points. Talent like this doesn't come around too often. This is his last game before the NBA draft in a couple of months. I think he's trying to show the pros what he's working with."

Cameras were positioned everywhere. From local

news stations to national coverage, every media outlet was there to witness Malek's last game of his high school career. He was considered the nation's top basketball recruit. The spectators jumped to their feet and roared with excitement every time he got the ball in his hands.

Everyone thought that Malek was showing out because it was his last game, but Halleigh knew the real motivation behind his extreme performance that night. After every basket he scored, he pointed to her in the stands.

"Girl, he's pointing at you." Nikki bumped Halleigh's shoulder as she sat there in the stands right next to her.

Halleigh cheered loudly throughout the game and admired her man as he brought the packed crowd to their feet time and time again. With every point he scored she thought, *I'm really about to give it up now. He's working hard for this.* She almost felt honored that her high school would have her to thank if they won tonight's game. A tremor of exhilaration mixed with fear frissoned up her back.

By the last few seconds of the game, Malek had managed 47 points and 15 assists, and his team had a 10-point lead. During his final moments on the floor, he simply dribbled the ball, showing off his handling skills as the crowd began to chant his name in unison. Malek scanned the crowd until his eyes met Halleigh's, and then he smiled at her as the final buzzer sounded off. The crowd went absolutely crazy as they rushed the floor.

Halleigh eventually made her way down to the

court, and Malek made a beeline over to her, by-passing all of the flocking reporters. Once he reached her, he picked her up and hugged her tightly, kissing her as he celebrated his team's championship victory.

"I love you," she whispered in his ear.

"I know," he said. "And I can't wait for you to show me just how much." Then he quickly ran back onto the floor to hoop and holler with his team.

Chapter Two

After the game, Halleigh leaned on Malek's beat-up Ford Tempo and waited patiently for him to exit the school.

One dude yelled, "Hal, tell Malek I said good game!"

"Yeah, he did his thang out there!" a girl added.

Halleigh smiled. "Yeah, he gon' be feeling thick tonight." She had to admit that Malek did play a good game. She was proud of him for everything that he was accomplishing and felt blessed to know that he'd chosen her to share his future with.

On the outside, Halleigh Walters looked like a regular, carefree teenager without a worry in the world, but on the inside, she had come up in a harsh environment. Growing up in a single-parent household, it had always been hard for her mother, Sharina, to take care and provide for her. Sharina had never had a real relationship with Halleigh's father, who never played a role in his daughter's life, so the sole support for Halleigh fell on her mother's shoulders.

In Halleigh's early years, Sharina had worked as a line worker at the General Motors plants. Many people say that shop jobs aren't meant for women because of the strenuous labor that comes with it, but Sharina did what she had to do to make ends meet. Making pretty decent money, she took care of Halleigh, and although her long work hours left Halleigh alone most of the time, they never needed for anything.

Unfortunately, Sharina had become another casualty of economics and was one of thousands to lose her job, when the hiring of cheap, overseas labor took its toll and General Motors decided to downsize their plants. General Motors was the livelihood of Flint, so the loss of these jobs hit everybody hard. If you worked in the shop, you lived a middle-class lifestyle. But for Halleigh, it seemed to have hit her mother the hardest.

Out of work, and depressed because she wasn't having any luck finding another job, Halleigh's mother fell victim to her circumstance, and ended up turning to drugs as her daughter sat by helplessly and watched. A strong drug habit quickly formed, and Sharina became addicted to heroin, which affected Halleigh's entire outlook on life.

Once unemployment and government assistance would no longer do the trick, instead of turning tricks herself, Sharina started boosting clothes, not to feed her daughter, but to feed her habit instead. But it was that same skill of boosting that Sharina had mastered that kept people from being able to tell just how bad Halleigh's upbringing really was.

Halleigh stayed fly in the latest fashions, because her mother's closet looked like the local Macy's. Sharina always made sure she boosted some nice pieces for both herself and her daughter. And just like a Mary Kay consultant, she had to be a representative of her product. In fact, Sharina was a walking advertisement for her craft. And for Halleigh, dressing nice was her way of hiding her predicament from the world.

Nobody knew how tough she had it. Nobody but Malek anyway. Halleigh tried to hide it from him at first, never allowing him to come to her house, making up the excuse that her mother would flip the script if she knew her baby girl had a boyfriend. But after a while, and after Halleigh ran out of excuses, he finally got her to keep it real and to tell him what was really going on at her house that was so bad that she didn't want him to be witness to it. The last thing Halleigh wanted her new man to know, her new man that lived in a house with both of his parents and dressed nice because both of his parents were employed, was that her mother was a drug addict whose occupation was stuffing pieces of clothing down a girdle.

But even when Halleigh confessed to Malek one night on the phone when he wanted to stop by and just see her, and her refusal led to a huge argument, his feelings for her didn't change. As a matter of fact, he was relieved. For some reason, he thought that Halleigh might have been ashamed of him, although he couldn't imagine why, or even worse, that she had another nigga that she didn't want to get busted with.

Malek loved her unconditionally and didn't look down on her because of how she had come up. He knew that her circumstance wasn't that uncommon. He truly admired and respected her. Even when his boys told him that he could do better than her, he begged to differ. Far from the prettiest girl in Flint, he thought she was the sweetest and most innocent girl he had ever been with and liked how she carried herself. He also liked a girl with some meat on her bones.

Malek definitely wasn't going to hold Halleigh's being poor against her. Hell, Flint was a dead city. Most of the people who lived there were poor, and not because they wanted to be, but because it was the only way to be. Flint had literally become a war zone.

With an 18% unemployment rate and the cost of living steadily rising, people from Flint developed a dog-eat-dog mentality. Everybody was out for self. It got so bad that people felt like if you were stupid enough to let somebody get you, then you deserved to get got. Crime swept over the city like a plague, and Flint became notorious as the murder capital.

Even the hustlers weren't getting it like they were supposed to, unless they had a good connect. Then it was a completely different story. A city where people were once proud to be called a "Flintstone," had quickly been transformed into a city where dreams were lost. Everybody who came up in Flint knew the game. Because of its ruthless atmosphere, the city produced some of the grimiest dudes, the sheistiest females, the most strategic hustlers, the baddest bitches, and the most talented authors. Whatever a person's game was, they were usually the best at it because survival depended on it.

In a city like that, how could Malek look down on Halleigh for being a part of the majority? Even his own parents struggled every now and then. Most folks were only a paycheck away from being homeless, so when an unexpected financial situation occurred, it hit everybody's pockets hard.

Malek's parents weren't rich by any means, but they had a roof over their heads, food on the table, and clothes on their backs. His father even ended up working two jobs to make sure that his family didn't go without anything, and his mother's paycheck as a nurse's aide helped too. And they stood on the hope that their son would make it in life; having the number one draft pick for a son added extra motivation, of course. They knew that their hard work would eventually pay off. And when it came to Halleigh, it could eventually pay off for her too.

Malek spotted Halleigh leaning up against his car. "You ready?"

Nervous energy filled her stomach when she saw him come out the building with a gym bag hanging from his shoulder. A Colgate smile was the only way to describe the look that was on his face.

"Y'all sho' look good together," an older man commented as he passed by. "Y'all make a nice-looking young couple."

"Thank you, sir," Halleigh replied, feeling like this was a good omen. They already looked like a settled young married couple. She couldn't wait until the day she said, "I do." She turned to Malek. "Yes, I'm ready."

Malek reached over and opened the passenger door for her, and she slid into the car. Then he drove off, blowing his horn for their victory at a couple of his teammates and fans.

Halleigh asked, "Babe, can you drop me off at home?"

Malek turned to her with a puzzled look on his face.

"I just want to freshen up a little bit. I've been sitting in there on those bleachers for the past couple of hours all sweated up and stuff." Though she'd never had sex before, she'd heard rumors about fishy-smelling chicks. And even though her hygiene was always up to par, she still wanted to make sure she was just right for her man.

Earlier, she wanted to pick up a throwaway douche for internal cleansing, but she decided against doing so. She didn't want her mother to find the box. As much as Sharina had deteriorated over the last couple of years due to her drug habit, Halleigh still gave her mother her respect.

Also, she didn't want to break her hymen. She'd heard that could happen from taking douches or using tampons. She wanted Malek to be the one to break her in. She wanted everything to be perfect.

Malek cruised the city streets until he finally made it to her house on the north end of town.

Before getting out of the car, Halleigh asked, "Are you sure your parents aren't coming home tonight?"

"Yeah, Moms won't be home until tomorrow morning. She's working the graveyard shift at the hospital tonight. My pops is on a business trip that he couldn't get out of, so we have the whole night to ourselves. I'll have you back home by the time my moms gets in. How about your mom?"

Halleigh shrugged. "You know her." Her mother was known to stay out all night and disappear at any given moment. She changed the subject. "You get the condoms? I don't want to get pregnant."

"Yeah, I got this. Don't worry, baby. "

Suddenly Betty Wright's song, "Tonight is the Night," came on the radio.

Malek glanced at Halleigh. "Baby, they playing our song. Tonight I'm-a make you a woman. And I will be gentle with you."

Halleigh didn't reply. The seriousness of her choice hit her. She'd no longer be a little girl. In fact, she was just moments away from being a woman.

As she reached for the door, Malek stopped her.

"You sure you down for this? I love you, Hal, and I want you more than anything in the world, but it's still your choice."

Halleigh thought for a minute. "Even the NBA?"

"Huh?"

"Do you want me more than going to the NBA?"

Malek leaned over and kissed her softly on the lips. "Even the NBA."

Halleigh hesitated, before nodding. "Yes, baby, I'm sure that I'm down for this." She opened the car door.

"You want me to wait for you or what?"

Halleigh looked over to her man before stepping out of the car and going into her house. "No, baby, you've waited for me long enough. I'll be over in an hour."

Chapter Three

Halleigh sauntered into her house and headed straight to her bedroom. She looked around their two-bedroom bungalow but didn't see her mother. "Dang!" she groaned.

The house was so cluttered, it looked like a cyclone had hit it. Their current housekeeping standards were lower than when her mother used to work sixty hours a week in the plant. Then, her mother kept a cleaner, more organized house than she did now. Seems like she would have had all the time in the world to clean now that she didn't hold down a job, but that would have been too much like right. Instead, the house looked like she had turned it upside down looking for a hit.

Halleigh had to admit that she kept her room on point. It was the rest of the house that was an embarrassment. No matter how much Halleigh cleaned, Sharina and her junkie friends would come in behind her hard work, filling ashtrays and leaving beer bottles and drug paraphernalia lying around the house.

At first, Halleigh would just continue to do the best she could to clean up again, but her mother would run through the house during the day while she was at school and tear everything back up, looking for any loose change to cop some more junk. After a while, Halleigh came to the conclusion that her efforts to keep the place looking even halfway decent were in vain, so she didn't even like to invite Malek over anymore. Tonight, though, Halleigh decided to ignore the disarray and just get ready for her intimate evening with Malek.

She opened up her panty drawer to see what she would wear that night. Even though, as Betty Wright would tell it, tonight Malek was going to make her a woman, as a high schooler, she didn't have anything along the lines of lingerie. She figured that a cute bra-and-panty set would have to do the trick. Since black was sexy, she picked out a black one her mother had boosted from Victoria's Secret. She also picked out a short denim Azzure skirt and a blue shirt that hung loosely off her shoulders.

Relieved that her mother wasn't home, she figured, once she was already gone, that her mother wouldn't miss her presence, so she hurried into the bathroom to take a shower. The water felt good on her skin, as she thought about the way that she was about to give herself to Malek; her nipples hardening and tingling from the hot water pelting them. Though extremely nervous, she got excited just thinking about her man and how she was going to become a woman. Malek's woman. Would it hurt? She'd heard from Nikki that the first time hurt, and that sometimes the girl would even bleed. Her vagina contracted, just thinking of it. Would she enjoy sex as much as she enjoyed just spending time with Malek?

The funny thing was that her body had been craving and wanting to have sex with Malek for the past few months, but her mind always gave her hands the order to push him away, once he tried to go beyond her bra or panties. She would allow him to kiss her, but never go too far. No grinding, no dry sex, no fingering, no titty-fucking. None of that stuff high school kids made famous. And he seemed to respect her all the more for setting this boundary.

In the past, Malek had told her he'd been with a lot of "technical virgins," who would let him finger them, or who would even do blowjobs on him, just so they could still claim they were virgins. But Halleigh . . . now that girl truly was a virgin. She'd never even masturbated.

Oddly enough, Halleigh wasn't raised to put a premium on being a virgin when she got married. In fact, before her mother got on the drugs, the only warning she used to give her daughter regarding sex was just to make sure her first time was special. That it should be with someone she loved. Sharina had also told Halleigh to come to her and inform her when she was ready to become sexually active so she could put her on birth control pills. Her mother used to be cool like that. In fact, before Sharina became addicted, she used to take relatively good care of Halleigh. Now, it seemed Halleigh had to take care of her.

Nowadays, the truth be known, Sharina didn't care what her daughter did. If Halleigh hadn't disciplined herself, she could really have run the streets wild. That's why it wouldn't be any problem to spend most of the night over at Malek's house tonight. Sometimes, she didn't like to think about how different her once-caring mother had become, but tonight she would use it to her advantage.

The good thing that came out of a bad situation was that after her mother got on drugs, Halleigh started wanting a better life for herself. She saw what happened when you gave up on life and didn't practice self-control. At seventeen, unlike many of the youths she'd grown up with, she'd never smoked, drank, or tried any type of drugs. And she truly didn't want to be another teen mother, like so many of the girls in her neighborhood, so she'd purposely abstained from having sex. It never swayed her that many of her friends had been having sex since they were twelve.

After rinsing the soap off her body, Halleigh exited the shower, not wanting to escape from the steady massage of the running water. Next, she sprayed on some of her mother's *Incidence* perfume that she had lifted from the Genesee Valley Shopping Center. Then she stood in front of the mirror and carefully shaved her na-na. She'd read about this in magazines and wanted to tame the hairs running wild between her young legs. She sprayed the scent on her neatly trimmed vagina and applied a sweet-scented body lotion from head to foot.

The sound of the door slamming made her jump. *Damn! Now I got to lie about where I'm going,* Halleigh thought. *I'll just tell her that I'm staying the night at Nikki's crib.* She exited the bathroom and proceeded to get dressed. "Hey, Ma!" she yelled as she dressed, but she got no response.

"Ma!" she yelled again. *I know she heard me.* She finished putting on her clothes and then made her way to her mother's room down the hallway from hers. When she opened the bedroom door, her mother was holding a soiled brown paper bag and frantically looking for a place to hide it.

"What are you doing, Ma?"

"Nothin', baby. Just go in your room." Her mother's eyes darted around the room. "Go back to your room." She quickly pushed Halleigh out of her bedroom and closed the door in her face.

Sharina seemed nervous, but Halleigh was too preoccupied to worry about her. Nowadays her mother always acted skittish, so she was used to her strange behavior of either being in a trying-to-get-high mode, or in an already high nod. There was no in-between. Tonight, though, she was glad that her mother had other things on her mind. *It shouldn't be too hard to get out of the house. She ain't paying me no mind, anyway.* Halleigh made her way back to her room.

A few minutes after Halleigh went into her room, closing the door behind her, a loud crash echoed throughout the house. It sounded as if it had come from the living room. She heard a male voice shout, "Bitch, you gon' try to steal from me?"

"No, Riq, it wasn't me," her mother pleaded. "You know I wouldn't take nothing from you, Riq."

The sound of her mother's screams alarmed Halleigh. She opened her bedroom door and followed the ruckus into the living room. "Ma!" she yelled, seeing two men beating on her mother. "Stop it!" Halleigh cried. "Ma!"

Startled, the two men paused from their beatdown on Sharina and looked in Halleigh's direction. They didn't even seem to consider that someone else could have been in the house. A twisted smile formed on one guy's face. He left his accomplice, who had Sharina pinned up against the wall by the throat, and approached Halleigh herself.

Sharina called out to the guy who was approaching her daughter. "Tariq," she said, calling the man by his full name, "leave her alone. That's my baby. She's only seventeen!"

"That's old enough to pay back your debt." Riq then turned to his partner. "Mad Dog, can you help?"

Sharina, palms held up in appeal, turned to look at Mad Dog, who was busy eyeballing the fresh meat that stood before them. Lust already shining in his eyes, he held his hand up in the "talk-to-the-hand" sign and shook his head, letting Riq know that he was down for it.

Riq began backing Halleigh up in a corner, his hands roaming all over her young body. He pressed his hardening manhood against her.

"Ma!" Halleigh cried.

Riq turned and looked over his shoulder at Sharina, while he continued to fondle her daughter's body. "What's it gon' be, Sharina? You can either give me back my package with interest, or you can let me fuck your daughter here and we'll call it even." Riq put his hands up Halleigh's short skirt.

Sharina thought about the monkey that was on her back. She had an entire package that would take her into ecstasy. There would be no way she would be able to feed her habit if she gave it back to him. *Halleigh is about to be a woman anyway. It's not like he gon' hurt her,* Sharina thought selfishly. *Besides, even if I do give the package back, their dicks are already hard. They probably gonna do her anyway.*

"Mama, please, make him stop!" Halleigh screamed, snapping Sharina out of her thoughts. "Maaaaaa!" she wailed, as the tears glistened and fell from her eyes.

"What's it gon' be, Rina?" Riq asked, rubbing himself.

"That's my baby, Riq." Sharina figured she'd give one last-ditch effort to save her daughter from the pending sexual attack.

"Okay. Then where's my shit?"

"Like I said, I don't—"

Before Sharina could even finish her sentence, Riq's partner punched her in her lying mouth, spilling blood and loosening teeth.

Sharina held up her hands to block the oncoming blows, but it was useless. She began to see stars, and her head began to pound and throb. She knew if she didn't do something quick, one of those blows would be fatal. One of her eyes had already swollen shut and was filled with blood. With her other eye, when she didn't see a fist coming toward it, she saw her daughter standing in complete fear of a rampaging Riq. At that moment, she knew what she had to do.

"Okay, okay! Wait!" Sharina held up her hand. "I don't have your money, but"—she saw the same fist that had been beating her mercilessly making its way toward her again—"but you can have her instead," she quickly shouted, halting the fist before it landed on her flesh.

Riq looked from Sharina to her daughter, who was standing there all dressed up as if she knew tonight she would have a debt to pay for her mother. Halleigh looked at her mother in shock. She couldn't believe the words that had just come out of her mouth. No! She had to be hearing things. No!

But when Sharina took one last look at her daughter with apologetic eyes, and then put her head down as not to witness the rape of her own child, Halleigh knew she'd heard right. Her instincts told her to do one thing—run like hell!

She took off for the door, but Riq caught her

and tackled her to the hard floor. "Uh-uh, sweetness. Where you think you going?" He forced his hands up her skirt.

Halleigh could feel his fingers invading her space. Her jaws tightened as she cringed in pain. "Ma!" Halleigh cried out in anguish as she fought back by beating Riq on his back. That was all she could do, with the weight of his body pinning her to the ground.

"Shut up!" Riq ordered as he brought his open hand down across her face. She clawed and kicked, but when his accomplice came and helped him hold her down, she was overpowered and didn't have a chance in the world to escape their clutches.

They were about to take, in an instant, what she'd made Malek wait for for years. Her virginity was what had made her different from the other girls to him. It was what made her special. Moreover, it was what had made their relationship valuable to both of them. She just couldn't let them take what wasn't theirs. She just couldn't.

Halleigh took a deep breath and tried with all of her might to loose herself from the grip of her attacker. The next thing she knew, Mad Dog spread and held her legs apart, while Riq pinned her hands behind her head. With one hard shove, Riq penetrated her, plowing into her young body as though she were a seasoned hooker. Once inside her narrow canal, the drug dealer took long, hard strokes.

Halleigh must have blacked out because, when she came to, suddenly she saw herself drifting near the top of the ceiling, looking down on the two men going at her body like two rapacious vultures picking over a dead carcass. Halleigh could have sworn she was having an out-of-body experience, but she was in such pain. Although she knew it was herself lying there, she hurt so badly, she became this disembodied figure, floating above the men's sexual assault, to be able to endure it.

Dispassionately, she looked down from the ceiling and watched Riq, pants wiggled down below his hips, hump up and down, up and down, like a disjointed caterpillar.

"Oooh, buddy," he gasped between moans, "this shit is tight. I mean, damn, it's good. This young girl know she got some good-ass pussy."

Still holding Halleigh's legs apart, Mad Dog licked his lips salaciously. "Oooh, hurry up, man, so I can get some of that sweet young stuff."

Finally, Riq shuddered and let out a loud groan of pleasure. "Owwww!" He collapsed on top of Halleigh and heaved deep breaths.

Mad Dawg pulled out his erected manhood. "Dawg, get the fuck up so I can get mines."

Pushing his penis back into his pants, Tariq stood up. "Eee-ooo-wee! That cherry was in there so tight. I'm already sore. But, man, that was the best cherry I ever busted." He looked down at the blood between Halleigh's legs. Her eyes were glazed. She appeared to be semi-conscious at this point. He scratched his head in disbelief. "I didn't think they made no virgins over ten around here no more."

Both he and Mad Dog shared a laugh.

"Well, I guess I'll just help break her in some more." Mad Dog rushed in and climbed on top of Halleigh, and she passed out again.

When she came to, he had turned her over and was sodomizing her. When he got through, Riq took another turn, all of this while Sharina had snuck off to the bedroom to get high.

Sharina had never thought her habit would push her to do something so horrible as to trade her very own flesh and blood for a fix. It was so awful, she couldn't bear to watch them take her daughter's innocence. That's when she went into her room, removed the package from her closet, and wrapped a leather belt around her arm, ignoring Halleigh's screams. She hurriedly put the heroin into a tablespoon and lit a flame to it, causing the contents to melt down. She filled the syringe and located a large vein.

When she felt the drug go into her system, she knew that her decision was well worth it. *Shit, Halleigh will be all right. Truth be told, she was probably already fucking anyway.*

Sharina didn't even realize how much damage she had just caused. The last thing she heard before drifting into a nod was the sound of Halleigh calling her name over and over again as the two men brutally raped her.

Chapter Four

A barefoot Halleigh, crying her young eyes out, stumbled aimlessly down the street. In throbbing pain, she gripped her hand over her stomach. She felt like her coochie and her ass were both going to fall out and hit the ground. The streets were deserted, and she'd never felt more alone in her life. Feeling discombobulated, she could hardly see because she was so blinded by her own tears.

"I can't believe this just happened to me," she muttered to herself. *This has to be a nightmare,* she tried to convince herself, but the pain that she clearly felt proved otherwise. This couldn't be happening to Halleigh. This wasn't the night's plan. She was supposed to be wrapped up in Malek's arms, but then the sound of her feet scraping the glass-splattered, needle-scattered sidewalk of the empty street would bring her back to reality. This was really happening, and it was happening to her.

Her innocence had been viciously stripped from her at the expense of her mother's drug habit. Her womanhood ached and bled under her skirt as she headed towards Malek's house. She didn't know where else to go. He was the only one that she could ever confide in; the only one who ever made her feel loved and protected. She had to get to him.

Once upon a time it was her mother who she felt she could confide in, who could protect her, but that was a thing of the past. She couldn't believe that her mother had just tricked her out, and as badly as that betrayal cut her to the bone and had her body wracked with pain, her heart ached the most. Who could a girl trust if she couldn't trust her own mother?

She'd never felt more desolate in her life, walking through the only city she'd known as home. Flint's streets were so cold, in more ways than one, and the streets were pitch-black, because the city's hoodlums had busted out the streetlights.

As the thoughts of those two grown men taking turns with her body would revisit Halleigh's mind, she would mumble, "No, no, no," over and over as she shook her head. She felt so defiled. So humiliated. So cheated. She kept thinking about what she and Malek could have had tonight, if only the rape hadn't happened. Those men could have taken anything in the house, the TV, the DVD, the CD player, which were the only things of value they had left that her mother hadn't already hocked. Those were material items that could have easily been replaced. But instead they chose to take something that was irreplaceable. Something Halleigh could never get back.

What she and Malek would have had would have been so innocent. So pure. So unlike from what she'd experienced with those two animals whom she felt had pissed in and on her. They not only robbed her of her innocence, but in so doing, they had stolen her right to choose. The two men had taken turns, both turning deaf ears to her pleas and ignoring her tears of outrage over being violated.

They didn't care that she had saved herself all these years for the man she loved. All they wanted was to fulfill their own lustful desires. To think she'd waited seventeen years for it to all wind up like this. Now she was just another ghetto statistic.

Suddenly a fine drizzle began to fall and quickly turned into large raindrops, which blended into Halleigh's tears. Oblivious to the rain swirling around her, Halleigh pushed forward with one destination in mind.

As soon as she approached Malek's small, Cape Cod-style house, she began to cry even harder. When she made it to his doorstep, she stood still for a moment before knocking. What should she say? What would she do? Would he even believe her? She weighed her options. Should she just go back home and pretend this whole thing never happened and try to just move on, or should she stay? But what if Malek tried to make her call the police and tell them what happened? What would happen to her mother? Would they take her to jail too for allowing it to happen? Then where would that leave Halleigh? Where would she go? To a foster home for someone to turn around and abuse her again? But what if she went back home and Riq and Mad Dog were still waiting to repeat the entire act all over again?

Absently, Halleigh shook her head. She was too afraid Tariq and Mad Dog might come back, and she never wanted to experience that again. She felt both embarrassed and abandoned as she contemplated knocking on her boyfriend's door. *Will he look down on me for this?* she thought as she stood there, drenched and shivering from the cold rain that fell from the black sky.

Finally, she made up her mind. Malek was all she had. She knew deep in her heart that he would be there for her. He had never looked down on her, so why would he start now? She knocked on the door and crossed her arms tightly around her stomach, her head down.

Seconds later, Malek opened the door, and the sounds of Usher lightly played in the background. Halleigh's knees buckled, and she fell into his arms.

Right away, he knew there was something wrong. Halleigh was crying, her hair was soaking wet, and her shirt was torn. He gently grabbed her by the shoulders and pulled her inside, closing the door behind them. "What's wrong, baby?" He held her against his chest. "Talk to me, Hal."

But she couldn't speak. She only cried.

Malek pulled her away from him, and his heart nearly dropped when she looked him in the eyes.

They were filled with humiliation, anguish, and pain. Her tears were flowing, and he could feel her body trembling. "Hal, what's wrong?" he asked again.

"They raped me, Malek," she said in a low voice inbetween her cries, a tremor rippling through her body.

"Whaaaat?" Malek stuttered. He wasn't sure he'd heard her right.

"They raped me." She embraced him and buried her head in his chest.

"Who? What? I mean . . ." Malek's words trailed off. He couldn't believe what he was hearing. "What happened, Halleigh? Who did this to you?"

Halleigh's mouth opened, but no words came out.

For a minute, Malek didn't realize that he was shaking his girlfriend. He was angry and seemed like he was going to lose his temper. Then he pulled himself into check and just shook his head. He wrapped his arms around her and hugged her tightly, never wanting to let her go. He was confused and angry at the same time. He was at a loss for words and didn't know what to say to her. His fist clenched tightly as he thought about someone hurting her. Her heartbeat began to pick up as he rocked her back and forth in his arms.

Finally he released her. "Who touched you, Halleigh?" he questioned again, but all Halleigh did was cry. "Who?" he shouted, frustrated with not knowing who had done this to his girl. He grabbed her by the shoulders and peered into her eyes.

Halleigh was so distraught, she just couldn't answer him. Her hysterical cries muffled her speech.

"Come on." Malek guided her over to the couch and sat her down to console her.

After finally getting her calmed down, Halleigh was able to tell Malek everything that had gone down back at her house. It brought tears to his eyes. He continued to hug her for the longest.

After a while, he broke his embrace then went to the bathroom and ran a tub of hot water. He helped his girlfriend into the bathroom and aided her in easing off her bloody skirt and underwear. Slowly, he helped her ease down into the tub. Fresh tears filled his eyes when he saw the water between Halleigh's legs and behind her turn red with her blood. He could see the bruises on her back and around her neck, but they weren't open wounds. He knew, without Halleigh saying a word, that she was bleeding vaginally and from her anus. He knew this wasn't menstrual blood. Once again, Malek just shook his head as tears fell. Tears of anger. He wanted to take somebody's head off, but first he knew he had to tend to a broken and bruised Halleigh.

Although they had planned to use a condom, they had also planned to have sex at the safest time in her cycle. She'd just had her period the weekend before. Plus, he'd never doubted that Halleigh had been a virgin before these animals took what rightfully should have been hers to give to whoever she chose.

What kind of men would take turns raping a young

girl? he wondered. Malek had never had to force any girl to have sex with him. And, as horny as Halleigh used to get him when they kissed, he'd never tried to take advantage of her against her will. Tonight, when his girl had finally been willing to have sex with him, the only way he would've wanted it, these animals seemed like they'd gotten off on forcing their way on her.

He gently sponged Halleigh's body and spoke in a low, hushed tone. "You're safe now, baby. I'm here. You're safe."

Halleigh could smell Malek's cologne, but it wasn't strong enough to cover the smell that had seemed to dwell in her nostrils. She couldn't stand the smell. The smell of the men's nasty sperm mixed with her blood. It smelled worse than when she was on her cycle. She started crying all over again.

"Shhhh. Don't cry, baby. Everything's gonna be all right."

Even though it was the first time Malek had ever seen Halleigh naked, he didn't think of anything sensual. In fact, sex was the last thing on his mind. He just wanted to soothe her and be there for her.

Halleigh had no shame in her nudeness either, and it almost seemed like a bad dream to her as she kept visualizing herself being raped.

Malek slowly rubbed his hands through her hair while she sat in the tub. He wanted to call the police, but in Flint the police were just as crooked as the criminals they chased down. Contacting them would only bring doom to themselves.

And the same thoughts that had crossed Halleigh's mind while she stood on the porch contemplating her next move crossed his mind too. What if they took her mother to jail? Then where would that leave Halleigh? Where would that leave him and her? At this point, Malek was just ready to take Halleigh as far away from Flint as possible and take care of her.

"Hal, I swear I'm going to get you away from all of this. I'm going to enter the draft, and you won't have to worry about anything. I won't let anything like this happen to you again," Malek said with confidence.

Halleigh looked up into his sincere eyes. "You promise?"

He wiped a streaming tear from her cheek. "I promise."

After the bath, he wrapped her in a large bath towel. He found one of his T-shirts for her to put on. "Here, put this on then come on and lay down," he said, pulling back the spread on his twin bed. "You need to sleep."

Still dazed, Halleigh lumbered into the bed. They didn't speak, they just laid in each other's arms, wanting to shut out the world. They lay on top of the bed like that for hours, and he could feel her pain as he held her in his arms.

Malek held Halleigh all through the night and watched her as she cried herself to sleep. He himself fell asleep with her spooned in his arms and didn't wake up until he heard a familiar voice screaming at him.

"Malek Lamont Johnson, what in the name of God is going on here?"

Malek sat up with a startled look on his face. It was early morning already, and his mother was off work and standing over his bed, a look of shock and disgust on her face. She had come in from work and found a half-naked girl and her son laid up. The fact that Halleigh wore a T-shirt didn't mean anything, because her bare breasts and nipples protruded beneath the shirt.

"Boy, I know you ain't got some li'l heifer laid up in my house!" She put both of her hands on her hips. "I know you must be out of your mind. What do you think your father is going to say about this?"

When she recognized the girl as Halleigh, she became even more upset. She'd never cared for Halleigh too much. Not that they were rolling in dough or anything, but she'd heard about Halleigh's upbringing and about her mother's habit and illegal career of boosting. She always thought that Halleigh just wanted Malek because of his potential NBA future, and like any mother, she was just being protective of her only child.

Malek was completely taken off guard, and before he could even respond, his mother began yelling again, forcing Halleigh to rustle out of her sleep.

"This is a house of God. I will not allow you to disrespect me up in here." Mrs. Johnson then focused her attention on Halleigh. "And you, you li'l fast wench, up in here half-naked, trying to trap my baby, get out!"

"Momma, hold up. It's not what it looked like. Calm down for a sec." Malek pleaded as his mother hollered, quoting Bible scriptures at the top of her lungs.

Halleigh was so embarrassed, so lost, and so confused. Even though she and Malek hadn't done anything sexually, she knew it didn't look good. While Malek was trying to calm his mother down, she just sat there, not knowing what to say.

Mrs. Johnson pointed her finger in Halleigh's face. "Get the hell out!"

"I'm so sorry, Mrs. Johnson."

But Mrs. Johnson wasn't trying to hear anything coming out of her mouth.

Halleigh got up, and with nothing on but the T-shirt, hurried out of the house while Malek and his mother argued.

Malek tried to run after her, but his mother blocked his path. As bad as he wanted to snatch his mother up and push her out of the way, he didn't.

Oh, my God, where am I going to go? Halleigh thought as she stood outside on Malek's porch and the reality sunk in further. She was too afraid to return to her mother's home. The truth of the matter was, she never wanted to return to her mother's house again in life. Sharina had gone too far this time. Malek was the only other person she had, so she just stood there, not knowing which way to go.

After a moment, she just began walking, and

just as she reached the sidewalk, Malek came darting out of the house running after her.

"Halleigh, Halleigh! Wait!" he said, clutching his Air Jordan shoes and running toward her. They both stood face to face with rain pouring down on them. "I love you, Halleigh. Just wait, let me calm my moms down. Let me tell her. Let me explain to her what happened."

"Malek, it's okay," Halleigh said, hopelessness filling her heart.

Just before Malek could respond, his mother stood in the doorway and yelled, "Malek, get back in here!"

He looked at his mother and then back at Halleigh. He didn't want to disobey his mother, but at the same time, he couldn't leave Halleigh. She needed him.

Then his mother went from quoting Bible scriptures to cursing. "Malek, get yo' ass in here now!"

Malek rarely heard his mother curse, so he knew she was upset. He froze up, looking back and forth from his mother to his girl.

Halleigh looked into his eyes. "Go on, Malek. I'll be okay." Then she kissed him on his lips and walked away. *There's nothing you can do for me anyway.*

Malek just stood there and watched Halleigh walk away. Hearing his mother yell his name again brought him out of his daze. Angrily, he trekked back to the front door and stood in front of his mother. "Ma, I can't leave her out here like this. I can't," he said almost in a whisper.

"You're going to pick some little ghetto girl to be disobedient over your own mother's word? Not even my word, but God's words. The Book of Proverbs says—"

"Ma, I don't care about the Book of Proverbs. I care about Halleigh."

Mrs. Johnson crossed her arms tightly and tapped her foot against the ground. "Okay, you wanna go running after some hoodrat? After all me and your daddy has done for you? After all we've sacrificed? Fine, go! As a matter of fact, you get out! You can go ahead with her. I work at all hours of the night and your father works two jobs trying to keep a roof over your head, and you got the audacity to even consider going against me! Get out!"

In a flurry of frenetic motion, his mother reached inside and grabbed his varsity jacket and hat and hurled them at him. With that, she slammed the door in his face, leaving Malek staring at the steel screen door.

But she knew her boy. She knew he wouldn't turn on everything his parents had done for him to go chasing after some panties, so she sat on the living room couch waiting, just knowing her son would come walking back through that door any second.

For a moment, Malek stood on the other side of the door like an ice statue. It hurt his heart to go against his mother's wishes, but he knew that Halleigh needed him more than ever. If only his mother knew why Halleigh needed him. He wanted to go back inside and make one last effort to explain to his mother what was going on. But when he finally willed himself to move, it was in the direction of Halleigh.

All those "suicides" his coach made him do were paying off now as he sprinted to catch up with Halleigh. Finally catching up with her, he ran up behind her, his sprints now long trots. "Halleigh! Halleigh!"

She turned around just in time to see her man approaching. "Oh, Malek," she said, touching his face. She was so glad and relieved to see him. "Thank you for letting me stay with you last night," she said. "I didn't mean to drag you into all of this." Her voice began to crack. "I just didn't have anywhere else to go."

"Everything is going to be all right." He wrapped his leather varsity coat around her shoulders. "Don't worry about it. I'm always here for you."

Hearing Malek's words and feeling his arms around her made her believe that everything, in fact, would be all right, but unfortunately it wouldn't

Chapter Five

It was around five-thirty AM, still pitch-black outside, and Malek and Halleigh trudged down the streets, wondering where they were going to crash. Malek knew that he could go back home if he wanted to, but he couldn't go and take Halleigh with him. But since he wasn't going to leave her hanging like that either, he decided to stay with her.

Halleigh definitely didn't want to go back to her mother's home. She'd rather sleep in the street or at a homeless shelter. What a joke! Her mother was no longer a parent who was there to guide and protect her as a young woman. Her mother had transmogrified into this walking-dead monster, who now saw Halleigh as a commodity she could exchange for her drugs. Halleigh sensed that if she went back home, the rape that had happened the night before was only a harbinger of what was to come at her mother's hands. Tariq and Mad Dog would only be the beginning of one long train of men her mother would bring in to use her body so that she could get her drugs for free. Hell no! Halleigh had to face the cold truth. Sharina's god wasn't the same god that Mrs. Johnson had been speaking of. Sharina's god was the heroin she shot in her veins. And what she had done to Halleigh was so foul, that her daughter could never forgive her for it.

As the couple made their way down the street, Malek thought about all his options as to where he and Halleigh could go. He thought about all the people who had been jocking him at school, but came up with nothing. There was no true friend whose house they could crash at. No teacher, no relative. He had no money, didn't have the keys to his car, and no plan. What were they going to do?

It was pouring rain and nearly thirty degrees outside. The two began shivering. The swirling rain lashed at both of their bodies, drenching them, as lightning flashed across the sky, the loud thunder frightening them.

Malek knew that they needed shelter or they would freeze to death. If only they had just a few dollars, they could surely find a cheap motel to crash at. They walked past the twenty-four-hour corner store on the corner of Clio Road, and Malek suddenly got an idea of just how they could get money.

* * *

Malek ran his plan by her. He stuck the small beer bottle under his shirt, pretending it was a gun.

Although Halleigh didn't agree that robbing the corner store was a good idea, she didn't have a better one. Here she was walking around half-naked. It would be daylight soon. They needed a place to stay. "Malek, you don't have to do this," she said.

"I'm just going to take enough for a hotel room for us, that's all. I promise. It'll be quick and easy." He kissed her on the cheek and went into the store with his hat pulled low over his eyes.

"Be careful," Halleigh whispered as Malek made his way to the door. She watched through the store's glass windows while she stood in the nearby alley. She wanted to stop Malek, but he was too determined to make sure they would be okay. Besides, what other options did they have? To go back and ask his mother to loan them some money for a hotel room? Yeah, right!

She watched as Malek slowly walked up in the empty store, an Asian man standing behind the counter, his hands in his hoody. Moments later, the Asian man put both of his hands in the air, a terrified look on his face. Halleigh knew that Malek had gone through with it.

Her heart began to pound, and her limbs shook as she watched Malek attempt to rob the owner with a beer bottle. She got a bad feeling in the pit of her stomach. A feeling that told her that Malek should just get the hell out of there right now—whether he had the money or not. "Just leave, Malek, please. Just leave," she whispered to herself as she watched the scene unfold.

Malek's hand began to shake. Obviously, he was nervous. Suddenly she saw both men turn their heads toward the back of the store as if they'd heard a startling noise or something. She turned her attention toward the direction both Malek and the Asian man was looking, and saw another store clerk come from out the back. The Asian man behind the counter reached under and pulled out a chrome handgun and pointed it toward Malek's head. By the time he turned back around, he was staring at the barrel of a gun.

Terrified, Halleigh barreled toward the store. Upon entering the bell hanging over the door rang.

Malek looked over at Halleigh, and just then a shot rang out as he tried to put his hands up to signal Halleigh to get out of the store. Boom!

A single bullet went through Malek's head. In one side and out the other. That was the last thing Halleigh saw before she saw his lifeless body drop to the ground.

"No!" Halleigh exclaimed, snapping back to reality from the horrible vision that had just played out in her head. She took a shuddering breath.

Malek stood in front of her, staring at her. He had the bottle tucked in his hoody. "What? What's wrong? It doesn't look like a real burner?" He looked down at the bottle. "You don't think I can pull this thing off with it?"

"Malek, I have a bad feeling about this one. Don't do it!" Halleigh held on to his arm, trying to persuade him not to go through with it. She kept visualizing her brief daydream of him being shot and didn't want it to become a reality.

Malek reconsidered the act he was about to commit. Thought about his NBA career for a moment, and how getting caught doing something like this could ruin his professional basketball career before it ever even took off. A Maurice Clarett he didn't want to be.

But every time he looked at Halleigh, she gave him the adrenaline he needed to do it. He'd promised her that he would take care of her, and now was the time for him to make good on his word. "Don't worry." He kissed her on the cheek and pulled away from her.

He pulled his hat low over his eyes as he went into the convenience store. He kept looking over his shoulder at the camera monitor lodged in the ceiling's right hand corner.

Feeling helpless, Halleigh looked on through the glass windows of the store as the scenario unfolded. Her heart began to pound, and her limbs shook as she watched Malek attempt to rob the storeowner with a beer bottle.

"Just leave, Malek, please. Just leave," she whispered to herself as she watched the scene unfold. She watched as Malek's hand began to shake, obviously he was nervous. Moments later she saw the Asian man empty the cash register and hand Malek the money from the drawer.

"Come on. Come on. Get out of there," she whispered urgently as if Malek could hear her. No sooner than she finished her sentence, a police car pulled up. Halleigh didn't know what to do. She acted on her first impulse.

"Help! Help, please," she screamed while running toward the officer, trying to divert his attention. "A man just attacked and robbed me in the alley. He stole my purse!"

The officer got out of the car with both of his hands in front of him, trying to calm Halleigh down. "Hold on, ma'am. Calm down. Where did he go?"

"That way!" She pointed in the opposite direction of the store. She peeked over at the store at the same time that Malek was coming out with a handful of money.

Suddenly a loud shotgun blast erupted, followed by the sound of shattered glass. The Asian man had reached for his weapon while Malek was escaping, the blast from the shotgun just missing Malek's head. Malek quickly ran toward Halleigh, not realizing she was talking to a cop.

Hearing the ruckus, the cop quickly ducked down and reached for his pistol. He saw Malek running with money in his hand and saw the Asian man running toward the front door with his weapon still in hand. He put two and two together—a young black man running out of a store with money in his hand and a storeowner brandishing a gun in hot pursuit. In his mind, Malek was already guilty. The officer pointed his service revolver to Malek's face. "Freeze, muthafucka! Put your hands where I can see them! Now!"

Malek halted. For a moment, he looked as stunned as a rabbit caught in a snare. Finally, realizing he could get shot in the back, or worse, shot numerous times by the trigger-happy cop, he put up his hands in surrender. He instantly looked over at Halleigh, who stood there with her hand over her mouth in an attempt to trap the wailing that wanted to escape her lips. Her boyfriend had almost been shot dead right before her eyes.

Malek let out a groan of regret for his dumb actions.

"Get outta here, miss!" the cop yelled to Halleigh, his gun pointed at Malek. "Back up!"

Halleigh didn't obey the officer's command.

"Ma'am, is this the man who attacked and robbed you?"

She just shook her head slowly. "No."

"Then go. Get out of here before you get hurt."

Halleigh looked into Malek's eyes and began to cry. Malek moved his eyes quickly, signaling her to go.

Halleigh didn't want to go, but she knew she couldn't do anything if she got arrested with him.

With his gun still aimed at Malek, the cop called for backup and then inched over to Malek. Once he reached Malek, he grabbed him and spun him around, hurtling Malek onto the ground, causing his head to hit the pavement forcefully. "You're under arrest," the police informed him. "You have the right to remain silent. Anything you say can and will be used against you. You have the right to—"

"Noo, what's happening?" Halleigh put both of her hands on her mouth as she cried out frantically. In a matter of hours she had gone from one bad nightmare to another.

Malek hissed at Halleigh, "Go! Get outta here!"

With his hands cuffed behind his back, he kept motioning for her to get away from the crime scene by jerking his head, which in turn, made his entire body jerk.

Which gave the officer grounds to say that Malek was resisting arrest. Suddenly the cop began to bludgeon Malek with his club to settle him down.

Guilt overcame Halleigh as she ran away, looking over her shoulder to see the cop beat Malek the way her mother had been beaten. She knew she was the cause of all of this. She should have just left Malek out of it. But it was too late. Now he was in far too deep.

Chapter Six

"Wait!" Halleigh screamed out as she ran out from the alley she had run down and hid in, but her calls went unheard, the police car driving away with Malek handcuffed in the back seat and damn near unconscious.

"Malek!" she called out once more at the top of her lungs. She didn't know if Malek heard her over the sirens or if he just felt her presence, but he slowly turned back and stared at her with haunting eyes. She watched the taillights turn the corner, her heart beating like a drum in her ear. She had no clue what to do. *They are probably taking him downtown,* she thought fearfully. She couldn't believe this was happening.

In spite of the hot bath, her body still ached as a result of being her mother's tradeoff. And her heart hurt from the thought of Malek being removed from her life by the law. Her mind hurt as she tried to think of a way to deal with the situation.

The only thing that she could think of doing was contacting Malek's mother. The fear of telling Mrs. Johnson that her son was in jail was enough to make Halleigh tremble.

At last, it had slowed raining and settled back into a soft drizzle, so she was relieved she wasn't out in the downpour as they had been earlier. She was still wearing Malek's jacket, but she was soaking wet from her head to her bare feet. Totally oblivious to how she looked though, she headed toward Malek's house.

When she arrived she could see Mrs. Johnson inside through the living room picture window. Mrs. Johnson's head was in her hands as she sat on the couch, and a wine glass sat on the table in front of her. Halleigh could tell that she was worried about her son. Filled with trepidation, Halleigh reluctantly marched up to the sidewalk that led to Malek's house. Her hands felt like they weighed a ton as she reached up and knocked on the door. Halleigh's breaths became hollow. She wanted to leave the doorstep, just as she had contemplated the night before.

Without warning, the door opened and Mrs. Johnson saw Halleigh standing there. His mother's cheeks were ashy from the many tears that had dried up on her face.

The sight of Halleigh standing in front of her brought fresh tears to Mrs. Johnson's eyes. "Where is my son?" she asked.

Halleigh couldn't speak. The cat had her tongue. She was in shock and was beginning to feel like Mrs. Johnson had been right all along, that she was indeed bad news for Malek.

"Halleigh, where is my son?" Mrs. Johnson asked, raising her voice a bit.

"He-he was arrested, Mrs. Johnson," she finally responded.

Mrs. Johnson's heart dropped to her stomach when the words left Halleigh's mouth. *Not my baby,* she thought as tears came to her eyes. "Arrested? Oh, Lord." Mrs. Johnson put her hand over her chest.

"They took him," Halleigh cried, staring in the eyes of the woman who had brought her only love into the world.

"Arrested?" Mrs. Johnson repeated. She looked at Halleigh, who had tears running down her face. Instead of feeling sorry for her, she felt angry. "I knew that you were bad news from the moment I laid eyes on you."

Mrs. Johnson's words cut like a knife, but Halleigh had to agree with Malek's mother's perception of her.

Mrs. Johnson began to pace back and forth. "I need to call his father." She grabbed her cell phone. "No, wait, I need to get my baby," she mumbled frantically as she grabbed her purse and keys. "I need to get my baby!" she screamed, just imagining what those Flint cops might be doing to her son.

Halleigh followed Mrs. Johnson to the car. As Mrs. Johnson went to the driver's side, Halleigh waited at the passenger side with her hand on the doorknob.

Mrs. Johnson looked at her like she was crazy. "Where do you think you're going?".

"Mrs. Johnson, please . . . I love him," Halleigh pleaded. "I need to go see about him. Please, Mrs. Johnson. After this, you never have to lay eyes on me again, but please . . . I just need to know that he's okay." Halleigh stood there biting down on her bottom lip in anticipation, her eyes begging Mrs. Johnson to just this once put her feeling for her aside.

"Listen to me, Halleigh. I don't even know what took place to land my son in jail, but my spirit of discernment tells me that you have everything to do with it. If I've said it before, I'll say it again— you are not good enough for my son. Malek has a future, and I am going to make sure that you're not a part of it." She paused then held her hand to her chest, as if overcome by so much emotion. She couldn't go on. Finally she growled through clenched teeth, "Stay away from him and this house before I hurt you, little girl." The look in Mrs. Johnson's eyes showed that her threat was not an idle one.

All of a sudden, Mrs. Johnson stormed around the car to the passenger side. Halleigh backed away from the car while putting her arms up, not knowing what this crazed woman was going to do to her.

"And give me back my son's jacket." With that, Mrs. Johnson snatched the jacket off Halleigh's back, pushed past her, and went and climbed into her vehicle. She backed out of the driveway, wheels squealing.

"Mrs. Johnson, please!" Halleigh begged as she ran after the car and pounded on the hood desperately. All she wanted to do was get to Malek, but Mrs. Johnson ignored her cries and sped away, leaving Halleigh behind.

"What's your name?" Officer Cornwell asked, a smug expression on his face. *These street thugs coming in here with their diamond necklaces and their fancy cars. Cocky sons of bitches, I hope we lock all of their drug-dealing asses up.* He watched Malek remove all of the personal items from his pockets. He tilted his head from left to right, getting a better look at Malek. *He looks familiar. He must be a repeat offender.*

Malek didn't respond to the officer. He'd barely heard a word that he had said. He couldn't stop thinking about Halleigh. *Where is she? I hope she's all right,* he thought. *I should've never taken her home after the game. But how was I to know? I mean, I knew that her moms was fiended out, but I never thought she would stoop so low as to turn her daughter over as payment to get high.* Even though he himself was in a bad position, Malek could only think about helping his Halleigh. He loved her that much. Her well-being came before his own.

"Name?" the white officer repeated loudly, pounding the top of the table to get the young kid's attention.

Malek looked up at the officer. "Malek Johnson."

"Malek Johnson?" It was at that moment that Officer Cornwell realized where he had seen the boy's face before. Malek Johnson was Flint Central's starting shooting guard and the biggest thing to hit basketball since LeBron James. *What the hell is he doing here?* he thought to himself.

After realizing that Malek wasn't the average stick-up kid, he figured he could get some money for allowing the reporters to get photographs of Malek while he was locked up. *This will be a helluva story,* Cornwell thought greedily to himself. He hurriedly processed him into the system and then handed him off to another officer so he could get busy. He picked up the phone and dialed the number to the local news stations. If Malek hadn't been well-known before, he was about to be now.

Chapter Seven

Mrs. Johnson parked her car in an illegal zone and hopped out as she ran into the police station as fast as she could. As soon as she slammed her door shut, her cell phone rang. "Hello?" she answered in a frantic tone.

Alex Wilson, Malek's agent, screamed into the phone, "Denise, what the hell is going on?"

"Alex, I can't talk to you right now. I'm busy."

"Not busy doing what you're supposed to be doing. All I asked you to do is make sure Malek graduates and keeps a clean image until the draft. He's out here knocking over fucking convenience stores?"

"How do you know what's going on?" she commented in confusion. "I'm in front of the police station now, but I don't even know exactly what's going on yet."

"Then obviously you haven't watched the early-morning news, seven o'clock edition," Alex told her. "Malek is the golden boy right now. Someone made a phone call and tipped off the news stations. Those vultures are probably on their way down to the station right now."

"Oh, no." Mrs. Johnson put her hand over her forehead. "Is this going to affect his chances of getting into the league?"

"If those news cameras get to Malek, there will be no league for him. They don't take too kindly to players coming out of high school with tarnished images. If the press gets the facts, Malek will be finished before he starts."

Mrs. Johnson hung up the phone and rushed into the police station. "I need to see my son," she stated to the white officer, whose badge identified him as Officer Cornwell. She had no idea that he was the officer who had checked Malek in and sold him out to the press.

"What's his name, ma'am?" he asked, feigning ignorance.

"Malek, uh, Malek Johnson," she whispered, looking around nervously for prying ears.

"Right this way." Officer Cornwell led her toward the visitors' room. He knew that Malek wasn't supposed to have any visitors, but he figured that the scene would make for some good pictures for the press and a big payday for himself.

He brought Malek out in handcuffs and sat him in the chair in front of his mother. "You've got fifteen minutes, ma'am," Officer Cornwell told Mrs. Johnson.

She nodded her head in acknowledgment, and he left the room. "Malek, son, baby," she cried as she placed his face in her hands and observed his bruises from the beating he had taken from the arresting officer.

The beating itself had looked more brutal than it actually was, and although right after he was handcuffed and thrown into the back of the squad car Malek felt as if he was about to go unconscious, most of that feeling derived from the fact that he was in shock that everything was going down.

"You all right?" Mrs. Johnson caressed his bruises and the slight knot on his head. "What happened? Why have they arrested you? What did you do?" The questions poured out of Mrs. Johnson's mouth one after the other.

"Yeah, Ma, I'm fine," he told her, pulling back his face from her hands. He then proceeded to tell her about the prior night's events that led to his arrest.

Mrs. Johnson stared at her son for a minute before taking her purse and letting him have one upside the head. "What the hell were you thinking, boy?" Malek flinched, but Mrs. Johnson whacked him one more time with her purse. "Do you know what this is going to do to your father? All of this for some whore who probably would have given it up to them, just like her mother, for a crack rock?"

Malek ignored his mother's insults against Halleigh. That was nothing new, and he had learned not to speak on it, not wanting to give his mother even more ammunition to spit. But he was concerned about what she'd said about his father. Malek imagined how his father would feel knowing that the son he had sacrificed so much for and raised to be a good man was now sitting in jail. "Does Dad know?"

"No, he doesn't know. I decided to wait and find out what was going on myself. It would break his heart . . ." Mrs. Johnson's words trailed off and tears trailed down her face.

"Please don't tell Dad about this, Ma. Everything is going to be all right. I'll be out before you know it."

"Well, not soon enough. Not before the whole world knows it."

Malek thought for a second. "How did you even know I was here?"

Mrs. Johnson sucked her teeth. "Your little girlfriend came and told me. The one I warned would bring you down." She looked her son up and down. "And just look at you."

"I know I messed up, Ma." Malek dropped his head in shame. "But it's not Halleigh's fault. Where is she anyway?"

"You don't need to be asking about her right now. I don't know where the little fast heifer is, but you are not to see her again. She is the last thing you should be worried about." Mrs. Johnson's voice was stern. "You're about to throw your entire life away on that gold-digger. She only wants you for the money, boy. Can't you see that?"

"You don't even know her," Malek said, defending his girlfriend. "You never even gave her the chance,

Ma. I love her. I know her. She doesn't care about any of this NBA stuff." He shook his head from side to side, scratching it in confusion.

He was right. Halleigh didn't care about all that NBA stuff, but he did. And for the first time, it was starting to set in that he could have ruined his chances at everything he had worked so hard for all through high school. "I messed up, Ma. What am I gon' do? I messed up," he kept repeating. Tears threatened to fall from his eyes. Holding his hands together in his handcuffs, he laced and unlaced his fingers nervously.

Mrs. Johnson was about to walk over and embrace her son. "Oh, son—"

The door suddenly clanged open. Right before them were flashes and clicks from ten different news cameras rushing into the room.

Mrs. Johnson immediately went over to her son and hugged him, turning his back against the camera crews in an attempt to shield him from them. "Malek, this is not good, baby," she whispered in his ear.

Malek buried his face down to shield his face from the reporters and their probing lenses.

"Your agent called me to inform me that if the press got wind of this little mishap, that your chances of getting drafted were over. Now look at what's happening," she said, her voice cracking. "Look at what's happening."

Mrs. Johnson couldn't hold in the river of tears that streamed out of her eyes. Nor could she tolerate the insensitiveness of the media. "And what are y'all looking at?" She screamed at the police officers who stood idly around the room and watched the drama unfold, "Get these reporters out of here!"

The cameras continued to flash in her son's face. She tried her best to shield him from them, but he had dug his own grave. She couldn't save him this time. The paparazzi were onto his scent. They smelled scandal and were as bloodthirsty as sharks.

Malek buried his chin in his chest, trying to hide his face, but that didn't stop the reporters from flashing away. Eventually, after Mrs. Johnson's continuous protesting, the officers got up and escorted Malek back to the bull pen.

As Officer Cornwell walked next to Malek, he couldn't have been more pleased with what he had done. He had a five-thousand-dollar check waiting on him from at least three different TV stations, just for giving them the tip. "Well, son, looks like you're a star." He chuckled.

Malek knew that Cornwell was the one who'd sold him out, just by the look on his face and the tone of his voice. He was eating this whole thing up.

Before he was thrown back into the pen, he decided to call Officer Cornwell on it. "Was it the money? How much did they offer you?"

"Excuse me, boy," Officer Cornwell said, not happy with Malek's knowing and accusing tone.

"If it was about the money, I would have given you double what they gave you just to keep your mouth shut."

His words rattled Officer Cornwell's feathers a bit, but he quickly regained his composure. After looking Malek up and down, he said, "Boy, right about now you ain't even got a quarter in your pocket. Otherwise, you wouldn't have been out trying to commit robbery. Which you know is a felony, right, son?" He let out a wicked chuckle to complement his grin and then walked away.

Under his breath Malek replied, "But I could have been worth millions."

Chapter Eight

Halleigh had walked for what seemed like hours in the freezing weather before she finally reached the large jailhouse building. She was exhausted, but she knew that she had to get to Malek. She just wanted to see him, to know that he was okay. She pulled her damp T-shirt down below her knees and entered the building.

"Are you okay, young lady?" an officer asked her as she entered through the Flint precinct's glass double doors. He couldn't help but notice her bare feet as his eyes stayed glued on them momentarily.

Halleigh followed the officer's eyes down to her own bare feet. She hadn't even realized she had been walking around barefoot all of this time. The fact that her shoes had come off during her kicking and trying to get away from the assailants quickly reminded her of the ordeal she had gone through. She shuddered at the thoughts. It was at that moment that she wanted to say to the officer, "No, I'm not okay. I've been raped," but she wasn't there for herself. She was there for Malek, the boy who might have lost everything because he was trying to be there for her.

Halleigh shook off the selfish thoughts of herself and replied to the officer, "I'm looking for my boyfriend," she said in an almost inaudible tone. "He was arrested earlier."

The officer took his position behind a desk and flicked on his computer. "What's his name?"

"Malek Johnson."

The officer didn't even need to finish typing in the name. The jail had been a circus ever since the young man had arrived. "We can't allow anyone else in to see Mr. Johnson," he stated firmly. "The next person that sees Mr. Johnson better have bail money."

"No! I need to get him out of here," she pleaded.

"Malek Johnson can't go anywhere until he sees a judge, which ain't gonna be until Monday morning. And I wouldn't be surprised if the judge sets his bail at a million dollars for the little stunt he pulled. Just imagine all those kids from the projects that looked up to "the pull." And this is how their role model pays them back." The officer shook his head. "Crying shame, crying shame." The officer began shuffling papers, dismissing Halleigh as if she wasn't important.

Halleigh put her hands over her face and sighed deeply as she tried to keep her composure.

The officer looked up and saw she was still

standing in front of him. He frowned in concern. "Young lady, how old are you anyway? Why are you up here like this by yourself?"

She lied as she walked away from the desk, "I'm grown." With nowhere to go, she found a seat in the waiting area.

"Seems to me someone as grown as yourself would at least be able to afford a pair of shoes then," he called out.

Halleigh didn't respond. She just sat there thinking, *I'll just stay here until Monday if I have to. I have to see Malek. I want to be here when he gets out.* In her heart she knew that she had no other place to go.

Taking pity on her, the officer approached her. "Here," he said, extending her a pair of jail-issued flip-flops, "at least put something on your feet."

"I'm tired of y'all pig mu'fuckas always locking a bitch up! Damn! Get on my nerves. Got me in this musty mu'fucka."

Halleigh had been leaned up against the precinct wall, trying to ease her mind, when the loud voice snapped her out of her restless sleep.

"Give me my shit!" The girl snatched her belongings from the officer sitting behind the desk. She sat down and pulled a pair of stilettos and some cheap jewelry out of the bag that the officer had given her. She put the shoes on her feet, applied her bracelets to her arm, and sashayed out the door. "Fuck y'all!" she yelled, slamming the door closed behind her.

After all the commotion died down, a female officer, the one who had just been handling the screaming woman, walked over to Halleigh. She had noticed that Halleigh had been there for quite a while now. "Excuse me, young lady, but can we help you with something?"

"I'm just waiting for Malek Johnson." Halleigh tried to sound grown-up and undaunted by authority.

"Well, you can't wait here . . . unless you want to get arrested for loitering."

Now she could see why that woman had been going off. These cops were jerks. As bad as Halleigh wanted to show her ass, the only words that came out of her mouth were, "Whatever." She sighed under her breath as she got up and left the station.

The late winter air was colder than normal. The weather had shifted from a slight drizzle, to a downpour, to a thunderous shower with lightning and everything. Heavy rain drops pelted against Halleigh's skin so hard, she felt like she was lost in a hailstorm. Here she was, standing outside wearing nothing, but the flimsy T-shirt. And the flip-flops on her feet were soaked and didn't keep her toes warm. She was freezing and didn't know where she could possibly go until Monday morning.

Then she heard a familiar voice say, "Damn, Tash! Come the fuck on!"

When she looked up, it was that same girl who had caused the commotion earlier in the police precinct. She was pacing, switching her hips back and forth as if she were trying to create some type of friction between her legs. She was fidgeting just to stay warm.

"Come on, Tash. It's cold out here," she complained to herself out loud. Just then she noticed Halleigh walking by. She held up her hand and halted her as if she were hailing a taxi cab. "Ay, yo, you got a light?" she asked Halleigh.

Halleigh shook her head.

"Fuck," the girl snapped.

Just then, Halleigh watched as the girl walked to a car that was parked on the side of the street, looked around to make sure no one was coming, and then tried the door, which opened. Halleigh peeped her surroundings nervously. *I know this girl is not breaking into a car right in front of the police station.*

The girl popped in the car lighter and stood outside the car waiting a couple minutes for it to heat up. She lit her cigarette and then quickly closed the door and took her place back on the street to wait for her ride.

The girl looked Halleigh up and down and noticed her disheveled appearance. "Damn, girl, what happened to you?"

"You don't even want to know," Halleigh replied, blowing hot air from her mouth into her hands.

"You waiting for a ride or something?" The girl puffed her cigarette.

"No. I don't know what I'm doing. My boyfriend is locked up. They talking about he has to wait until Monday to get a bail set." Halleigh looked defeated. "Even then, I don't know how I'm going to come up with that. He's in all of this mess because of me, trying to look out for me. I don't know what to do." Halleigh's hands dropped to her sides as the rain washed her tears away.

"Where you stay?"

Halleigh looked around. "Right now, where I stand. I just need a place to think. I have to figure out what I'm gon' do."

"Well, it's colder then a bitch out here," the girl commented. "You ain't gon' figure nothing out waiting outside, especially in this cold-ass rain." She sucked her teeth. "What's your name?"

"Halleigh."

"I'm Mimi." She noticed that Halleigh was shivering and took pity on the girl. "Look, girl, you can crash at my spot if you need to. At least for the night. My daddy will probably be able to help you out too. He can help you get your boy out of jail if you want him to."

Halleigh didn't know Mimi from the man on the moon, but as of now, she had officially run out of options. She figured that anything would be better than being on the streets, so she decided to accept Mimi's offer. "You sure your daddy won't mind?"

Mimi smirked and looked Halleigh up and down and then licked her lips. "Nah, he won't mind, trust me."

Halleigh stood next to Mimi on the street as they waited for Mimi's ride to pick them up. She didn't want to seem like a charity case, but she didn't have anywhere else to go. For a moment she thought about going to Nikki's house. Nikki had a single mother too, but her mother was more strict on Nikki than Halleigh's mother was on her. Nikki had the type of mother who made phone calls to make sure a situation was kosher. Halleigh couldn't go and stay for two nights at Nikki's without raising suspicion. Besides, she didn't want Nikki to know about the disasters that had happened to her and to Malek. She knew that, underneath, Nikki had envied their relationship, and she would be glad to know all their plans had been shipwrecked.

Malek was locked up, so of course, staying with him wasn't an option. And her mother was so strung-out that she had sacrificed her relationship with her daughter just to get high. Halleigh knew that she would never walk into her mother's house again. There was no repairing their relationship. *I hate her,* Halleigh thought, feeling bombarded with mixed emotions of hatred, anger, and disgust for her mother.

Mimi paced up and down Saginaw Street puffing on her cigarette. She kept looking up and down the block to see if her ride was nearing. She looked down at the girl that she had befriended and could tell that she was carrying a large burden on her shoulders. "Here, hit this. It'll calm your nerves." Mimi offered Halleigh a drag of her Newport.

Halleigh shook her head. "I don't smoke."

Mimi shrugged her shoulders and took a long pull of the nicotine as she continued to pace back and forth, her silver stilettos that laced up her slim legs clicking back and forth. She wore a short silver halter dress, and her hair was braided straight to the back, her extensions causing it to fall right above her butt. Baby hair rested along her edges.

"Where the hell is this girl at?" Mimi muttered impatiently.

"Are you sure this is all right? Your daddy won't mind it if I stay the night?" Halleigh furrowed her eyebrows together in worry. She pondered over her situation. Who was this woman whose father would allow her to bring a stranger home? He must be a nice man, or why would Mimi even offer to allow this?

Mimi looked her up and down again and smirked. "Nah, like I said before, he won't mind. My daddy will be happy to have you. He'll help you figure everything out." Mimi's last sentence was said in a sing-song tone.

Just as Halleigh was about to reply, a caramel-colored girl with long layered hair pulled up in a Toyota and honked the horn. "Mimi, get in!" she yelled.

Halleigh anxiously waited near the curb while Mimi strolled over to the car. "Come on, Hal," Mimi called.

Instantly Halleigh picked up on the fact that Mimi had already used her nickname, as if they were friends. As if she'd known her forever. A sense of security swept over Halleigh, like everything would be okay. She began taking steps toward the car.

"Mimi, get your ass in the car!" the girl shouted from inside the car just as she noticed Halleigh making her way over to the car too. "And where the fuck she think she going?"

Halleigh stopped in her tracks as she looked helplessly at Mimi.

"Tasha, chill! She needs our help. She needs to meet Daddy." Mimi spoke through clenched teeth.

Tasha peered out at the girl who was standing beside her car. It was obvious that the girl had been crying. Her eyes were red and puffy. She was shivering, and her arms were wrapped around herself as if she were afraid. "Tell her to get in," Tasha said with an attitude. Heaving a sigh of resignation, she put the car in drive.

"See, I told you everything would be cool. Get in," Mimi said to Halleigh as she opened the back door for her.

Halleigh got into the car and rode silently as she watched the city streets pass her by. She could feel Tasha's eyes on her as she glared at her from the rearview mirror. She kept feeling her stare and started feeling uncomfortable in the confinement of the car.

"You know Manolo about to trip on you, right?" Tasha asked as they pulled into the driveway of a ranch-style home on the city's South Side.

"He'll be cool once he sees what I got for him." Mimi shuffled dollars together from inside her purse.

The three girls exited the car and entered the house. There were several girls scattered throughout the house. Some were lounging in the large living room, others were getting dressed and rushing about as they prepared to leave, still others walked freely throughout the house wearing nothing but their underclothes. Most of them had high-perched breasts, smooth thighs without cellulite, and round cantaloupe-shaped hips. There appeared to be about five women in all.

"This your daddy's crib?" Halleigh asked, scanning the large rooms with wonder.

"Yeah, he probably in the back," Mimi replied.

Halleigh noticed Tasha roll her eyes as she followed them down a long hallway in the five-bedroom house. They entered the room, and Halleigh saw a tall, well-built man sitting in a recliner in the corner of the room and puffing on a blunt. The first thing that she noticed was his long, perfectly manicured fingernails.

"How did you get locked up?" was his first question as he stared directly at Mimi.

"It was all a misunderstanding, Daddy. I promise it will never happen again," Mimi replied. She didn't give him a chance to respond. She just rambled right into her next sentence. "This is my friend, Halleigh. I met her outside of the jail when I was waiting on slow-ass Tasha to come pick me up." Mimi stroked a piece of Halleigh's hair and then pushed it behind her ear. "She is in a bind right now, and I told her that you might be able to help her out."

The man didn't even look Halleigh's way. Instead, he looked at Tasha. "What do you think?"

She looked over at Halleigh and, once again, rolled her eyes. "I don't know." She shrugged. "But I guess it could be a good move." Tasha made her way over to the man and began to massage his defined shoulders. "What do you think?"

Mimi noticed the way he was now looking at Halleigh. It was the same look he gave her when she'd first met him, so she knew that it was a done deal. She had done good.

Slowly, without Halleigh even noticing, Mimi backed up and began to ease out of the room. Just as she was about to close the door, the man called out to her, "Mimi, you gon' work double to pay me back that bail money," never taking his eyes off Halleigh.

Damn, this mu'fucka could've let me slide since I brought his ass some fresh pussy. Niggas don't appreciate shit, I swear. Mimi walked out of the room without responding, and Tasha followed, leaving Halleigh in the room alone.

Now completely alone with this stranger and under his steely gaze, Halleigh pulled at the T-shirt that she wore, feeling uncomfortable in her own skin. She felt goose bumps rise on her arms. The room was smoky from the weed, and Halleigh could tell that he was as high as a kite.

"What did you say your name was?" he asked as he continued to smoke on his blunt.

"Halleigh," she replied, then took a gulp, trying to swallow the huge knot in her throat.

"Halleigh. Your name fits you." He looked at her high-yellow skin tone and licked his lips as if he could taste her. Yeah, Mimi had done good.

Being in the pimping game for over ten years Manolo knew a lost soul when he saw one. Halleigh's eyes revealed her sadness. He didn't know what path she had followed that brought her to his doorstep, but he knew that he was about to lead her in a new direction. His eyes admired the proportioned curves of her young body, and he had to mentally tame his dick down when he noticed her hard nipples poking through her T-shirt.

"So why do you need Manolo's help?" he asked, referring to himself in third person.

Her thoughts instantly went back to Malek, and tears came to her eyes.

Manolo nodded his head toward his bed. "Take your time, baby girl. Have a seat. I won't bite you, I promise."

Halleigh sat on the bed near his chair. "It's my boyfriend, Malek. He was arrested, and I need money to get him out."

"What they holding him for?" Manolo tapped the blunt against an ashtray that sat on a glass table beside him.

Although hesitant at first because she didn't just want to be telling this stranger all of her business, she knew that if she was going to get him to help her, that she needed to tell him everything. "He robbed a store . . . but he's not like that. He only did it because I needed the money." Halleigh even told Manolo about the awful attack that took place at her mother's house and why she couldn't go back there. In fact, she revealed everything that had occurred, up to the point of stepping foot in his house.

"Sounds to me like your boyfriend ain't gon' want

nothing to do with you when he gets out." Manolo knew to begin planting the seeds of doubt into this fresh soil. "Sitting in jail has a way of making people think about things. He's probably thinking about you right now and how you've probably fucked things up for him."

Manolo's words were harsh, but Halleigh wasn't about to kid herself. She knew there was plenty of truth to them, and that Malek probably was sitting in jail right now thinking how none of this would be happening had he never met her.

"Now I want to help you," Manolo continued, "but I've got to be truthful. I'm not a liar, so I'm gon' keep it gully with you."

Halleigh nodded eagerly, wondering what he would say next. Here she was traumatized, perhaps expecting a little empathy, but Manolo dished out anything but.

"I know you believe your man is probably just thinking it, but I'm going to tell you straight up— this is all your fault. If it wasn't for you, your man wouldn't be locked up right now."

Flabbergasted, Halleigh's mouth flew open. Manolo's words shocked her as sharply as an unexpected slap. With his harsh words, she began to let her tears flow freely. Believing it was all her fault was one thing, but hearing it was another.

Halleigh stood there doing what it seemed she'd been doing for the last twenty-four hours, crying. She was tired of crying though. Those tears weren't getting her anywhere. It was time to do something about the messy bed that was made.

"What do I do?" she asked, wiping her tears away roughly, as if she was angry at them for even falling from her eyes. But as quickly as she wiped them, more would fall.

Manolo stood up and began to help her wipe her tears away. He knew that he had her in the palm of his hand. His main agenda was to get a woman to become and remain his ho. He called that "the pimp's creed." Having taken advantage of some of the toughest bitches that Flint had ever bred, he knew this was going to be a piece of cake. He knew how to break a grown-ass woman down, so he knew it wouldn't be any problem with such a naïve teen.

"It's your fault that this happened, so you have to fix it," he told her. "How you fix it is up to you."

"But how can I fix it? Even when they set bail, I don't have the money to get him out. His parents work hard and everything, but it's not their fault he's in there, it's mine." Halleigh knew that if Malek's parents had to come up off that bail money, Mrs. Johnson would do everything in her power to see to it that Malek never saw her again, and she couldn't let that happen. Manolo was right. It was her fault. She had to come up with the bail money.

Manolo questioned Halleigh the same way Satan had questioned Eve in the garden. "You don't have any money?"

"I don't even have a roof over my head right now."

Manolo put his index finger to his chin and thought for a minute. "He's in for robbery, did you say?"

Halleigh nodded.

"Is this his first offense ever?"

Once again, Halleigh nodded.

"Let me see . . ." Manolo, with his street wisdom, figured out how much Malek's bail would probably be for a first-time offender. "Ten stacks," he finally said.

Halleigh hadn't the slightest idea what he was talking about. "Huh?"

"Ten thousand dollars. That's my estimate on what your boyfriend's bail is probably going to be." Manolo thought for another moment. "Yeah, that is a lot of money"—he looked back at Halleigh—"especially for a girl who has nothing."

Halleigh's head fell, her chin to her chest.

"I could help you get that money." Manolo was glad to see he had the girl's undivided attention again. "But it won't be easy. It'll take a couple days, but I think we could do it if you work hard," he stated, throwing out the bait.

Relieved, Halleigh said, "I'll do anything. I just want to fix this."

"You can even stay here until you find your own spot," he said, knowing Halleigh would accept the offer.

Truth was, Halleigh really didn't have a choice but to rest her head under his roof. Any ho that had ever worked for him always lived in his house. *My roof, my rules,* Manolo thought to himself. He felt that it was easier to control his girls if he knew their whereabouts at all times.

"Halleigh, why did you come to me for help?

Where are your people? I mean, I know the deal with your mom, but haven't you anyone else you can turn to?" Manolo wanted to make sure that she didn't have anybody that could come and save her from the life she was about to get into. He knew that there would come a time when she would want out. By that time he would make her feel so hopeless that she would think that he was the only one who cared about her.

"I don't have anybody. Malek is the only person I can count on." Halleigh lowered her head at the thought of her mother. *She let them rape me.*

He took her hand and lifted her to her feet. "You can count on me, Sunshine," he whispered softly in her ear as he wrapped his hands around her waist.

"Sunshine?" Halleigh stated.

"Yeah, Sunshine." Manolo looked deep into Halleigh's eyes. "When I look into your eyes, I see a rainstorm. There's been so much pain in your life, so much thunder, I know you've felt as though a black rain cloud has just been following you around."

Tears began to fall from Halleigh's eyes. Manolo couldn't have been more right. Not only had it been raining on her, literally, for the last twenty-four hours, but her entire life was like one bad, pouring-down shower in which the rain just wouldn't seem to let up.

"Well, the rain is about to dry up, and there'll be nothing but sunshine in your life from this day forward." He then embraced her like a father would a daughter.

Halleigh broke down in tears as she appreciated his embrace.

"Shhh. I will help you get what you need." Manolo began rocking her back and forth in his arms.

He had sucked her in so deep that she was hanging on to, and believing his every word. He spat out so many broken promises and manipulated her young mind to the point that she didn't even realize that his hands had found a comfortable place on her ass while he was grinding his crotch slowly against her.

"Shh, that's right. Get it all out, Sunshine," he repeated over and over again.

And just like Halleigh had once felt, only in Malek's arms, she felt that same way in Manolo's arms. Safe.

Chapter Nine

Malek took a seat on the same bench Jamaica Joe was sitting on. Everyone else in the bullpen was terrified of Joe, but Malek's mind was elsewhere. He didn't even have the energy to be terrified of a man. The only thing he was afraid of was what Halleigh could possibly be going through right now; not to mention what would become of his basketball career.

He didn't even notice that everyone else in the room kept their distance as they tried to avoid Joe. The truth was, he really didn't know who Jamaica Joe was or what he stood for. He'd heard of his reputation, but he'd never seen him in person.

As a single parent, his mother had done the best she could to shield him from the malevolent streets. Then when he was eight years old, she married his stepfather, who as far as Malek was concerned, was his father. Kind of like how Shaq feels about his stepfather.

It was Malek's stepfather who was behind his involvement in basketball camps every summer since he was nine years old. The camps not only developed his skills, but also contributed to him burning up a lot of energy. He was always too tired to get into trouble.

Over the past five years, while his friends were going to Maxey Boys Training School for juvenile offenders, Malek had been too busy dribbling basketballs to get involved in crime. There were generally male mentors at the camp who spoke out against young black men getting caught up in drug dealing, crime, or substance abuse.

Up until his arrest last night, Malek had never had any trouble with the law. Now he'd just turned eighteen. He wondered, with this being his first offense, if the judge would be lenient on him and give him probation. He sure didn't want a felony on his record. He wondered if this would affect his chances of getting into the NBA. What a mess he had made of things.

In disgust, Malek buried his face in the palms of his hands as he blocked everything out that was going on around him. He was so busy regretting his foolish acts, he was oblivious to all the noise and chatter of the jail cell. Even if he had gotten enough money from the robbery for a night at a hotel, then what? Would he have to keep knocking off corner stores to pay for additional nights? He hadn't even bothered to think that far in advance. All he was worried about at the time was Halleigh. Speaking of which, he was worried about her now.

Malek took a deep breath as he stared down at his feet. All of a sudden some words his stepfather had spoken to him some time ago came back to haunt him. *"You don't even know how much danger is out there in the streets. You don't want to be in the wrong place at the wrong time and wind up in jail or prison, which is no place for a Black man."* His father may not have been in the home as much as Malek would have liked him to be. He may not have been able to attend his basketball games as much as he wanted him to, but his love for Malek went without question. He had done nothing but work hard since marrying Malek's mother.

Before Malek was even two years old, his real father was shot dead in a drug deal gone bad. And in an unrelated incident, his stepfather's dad had been sentenced to life in jail for a murder that took place during a drug deal gone bad. Prior to their deaths, the men had played no role at all in their son's lives, choosing the streets over their own flesh and blood. So Mr. Johnson knew what it was like to need and desperately want a man in the home to teach him how to be a man. To teach him how to be a provider and to take care of his family the right way. And for that, Malek had the utmost respect for the man his mother married. The man he called Dad.

Once again, Malek sighed and shook his head thinking about what his father would possibly think about him if he saw him right now; sitting in a jail cell for robbery. A blitz of reporters suddenly stood on the opposite side of the bars, and cameras were flashing away once again. Once the word that Malek was in there leaked to the media, the reporters flocked to the jailhouse to get a photo of the jailed star, first to the visiting room with him and his mother, and now right there in the jail cell. They were relentless and wouldn't let up. "Not this shit again," Malek said. He put up his hands up to shield his face.

Jamaica Joe discreetly turned his back, trying to avoid being photographed. After three straight minutes of constant flashing, the second wave of reporters left satisfied.

The criminals and drunks in the bullpen began an uproar. In spite of the stench coming from the one backed-up toilet in the corner and the crowded conditions, they all felt as important and as special as a group of rappers, several even posing for the cameras. Others threw up gang signs. They'd never seen anything like it.

One particular Latino man was the first to speak to Malek. He wore a tight T-shirt over his ripped, muscular upper body and had at least ten tattoos on his neck alone. He was obviously intoxicated, and in his mind, for some reason, he felt that Malek thought he was better than the rest of them. Well, that's what he told himself. He didn't want to admit that it was pure jealousy that caused him to dislike Malek.

"You must be somebody important, huh?" the Latino man yelled across the room.

Malek looked around and then focused on the man. "You talking to me?" he asked, placing his index finger on his chest.

"Yeah, I'm talking to you," the Latino man yelled in a drunken slur. "I don't see no other bitches in here."

The other men began to laugh at his comment, gassing him up more. Malek stared at the man for a second to see if he was serious and then dropped his head in an attempt to ignore him. He ran his hands over top his head, feeling the ripples of the few waves in his hair that still remained in spite of the rain.

The man wasn't done with Malek though. He hated pretty boys and felt obligated to tell Malek about himself. He staggered over to Malek to give him a piece of his mind.

Before Malek even realized that the man was headed over his way, the Latino man was standing directly over him. "You's a ol' bitch-ass, pretty boy. Who the fuck is you anyway? You got these mu'-fuckas snapping photos and shit. You ain't nobody. You in here just like the rest of us. You ain't no better than none of us."

Malek looked up at the man, with a confused look at his face and thought, *What is this mu'fucka's problem?* He watched as the man swayed from side to side and struggled to keep his balance. "Look, man, I don't want any trouble, fam," Malek told him.

The man must have felt that Malek was trying to be disrespectful, because out of nowhere, he swung on him. But before the man could connect,

Malek moved to the side, causing the man to spin around and almost fall.

Malek quickly rose to his feet and caught the man with two swift punches. The man didn't know what hit him. Jamaica Joe slightly grinned as he stepped to the side to give the two men room to get their brawl on. Malek followed up with another punch, connecting with the man's nose.

The Latino man held his nose in agony as he fell flat on his back. Malek smiled when he realized how quickly he had dropped the man. But the smile quickly dropped when he saw two other Latinos, that closely resembled the man he had just beat down, emerge from the crowd. From the way the men were dressed alike, it was obvious that they were from the same gang or set.

"Aye, homes, you done fucked up," one of the men said just before he ran up on Malek.

Malek shifted his stance and put up his dukes. He kept his eyes steady, and he stood his ground, refusing to back down.

Jamaica Joe just sat back and watched as Malek showed no fear. *Li'l man got mad heart,* Joe thought to himself as he leaned against the brick wall.

The men in the bullpen gathered around the fight to witness the unexpected entertainment.

"Get him."

"Fuck him up, *hombre.*"

"Fight, fight," the sideliners instigated.

Just like the first man, Malek laid the second one down in a matter of seconds, without as much as a scratch on himself. And the second one didn't even seem to be as drunk as the first one. Now, both men lay on the ground next to each other.

The third Latino man sized Malek up and circled him as he contemplated the best way to get at Malek. His chest heaved up and down from trying to catch his breath. Malek was tired from the scuffle with the two previous men, but he didn't show it. He was ready to drop this one the same way he had dropped the rest. The first man that Malek dropped returned to his feet, blood dripping from his nose. He might have been injured, but he was still ready to fight. Malek was outnumbered at that point and prepared himself for the worst.

"That's enough," a calm voice said. It was Jamaica Joe. He had seen enough and respected Malek's braveness. "Leave li'l man alone," Joe demanded of the Latinos, not even respecting them enough to look at them.

The men's demeanor totally changed at Joe's request. They all dropped their fists as they looked at Joe nervously. It was evident that Joe had control of the situation, because the three Latino men weren't even focused on Malek anymore. They were worried about Jamaica Joe.

Malek, on the other hand, didn't drop his guard and was ready to knock out whoever ran up on him.

"Ay, Joe, I didn't know he wuz with chu," one of them said in broken English.

Malek balled up his fist, his adrenaline pumping. "Run up, nigga!"

As much as the Latino crew wanted to, they did

nothing. Malek finally realized why everyone was on the opposite side of the room from Joe when he first came in. They feared him.

"Joseph Holland!" the guard yelled as he approached the cell.

A middle-aged white man with a neat tailored suit walked alongside the guard. It was Jamaica Joe's attorney, Anderson Wallace, one of the most prestigious and sought-after attorneys in the Midwest.

File in hand, Wallace was noticeably upset. "Release my client immediately! This is preposterous!"

Jamaica Joe headed out of the cell after it was opened for him, but not before Malek called out to him, "Thanks."

Joe simply nodded his head in acknowledgment and exited the cell. Malek watched as the guard closed the steel gate behind Joe, and then he focused his attention back on the bullpen. He was sure that the Latino gang would try to finish what they'd started, but to Malek's surprise, they didn't do as much as look at him.

After an hour of keeping his eye on the gang, when he figured that they weren't going to try anything, Malek, once again, began to think about his current predicament. He knew he had acted on impulse by trying to knock over the convenience store; an impulse that could change his life forever. But what could he have done? What other choices did he have? Should he have gone and tried to retaliate against the drug dealers who raped his girl? Those type of people didn't play, and they would have come after both of them and probably killed them. Absently, he shook his head. He was caught in a quandary. What else could he have done? What was he going to do now? He dropped his head in defeat. His whole world was tumbling down. When it rains, it pours.

Chapter Ten

"What am I gon' do?" Halleigh asked aloud. She was sitting in the bedroom that she now shared with Mimi. The room was just big enough to fit two twin beds inside, but she was grateful just to have a place to lay her head. She had taken a shower, and Mimi had loaned her some of her old clothes.

Manolo had told Halleigh that she could stay as long as she needed to, and he had assured her that he would help her make the money she needed to get Malek out of jail. The fact that she still had four more months of high school crept into her thoughts. How on God's earth was she going to be able to get back and forth from school, let alone, be able to focus on things once she was back at school? After a couple of minutes of sifting a few options and ideas, she decided that she couldn't worry about that now. Perhaps she could go back to school once she got a job and saved up some money.

Mimi sat on her bed with her back against the wall, painting her toe nails. "How much did you say ol' boy's bail is probably going to be?"

"Ten thousand," Halleigh replied.

"Damn! He gon' rot in that mu'fucka." Mimi let out a low whistle. "He ain't got no family that can get him out?" she asked. "I wouldn't be spending my hard-earned money on nobody's bail. His family would be going half or something." Mimi blew on her toes, attempting to dry the wet paint.

"His moms don't like me. She can't stand me. She won't even talk to me, so I don't know what is going on. His pops, I don't even know if he knows what went down yet. He was out of town for his job. He's always out of town working hard."

"Good. Then let his hardworking ass pay the bail, and you hit the Genesee Mall and go shopping."

Halleigh just shrugged her shoulders. She had already decided that she couldn't put that burden on Malek's parents' shoulders. Her heart was heavy, and whenever she thought about Malek sitting locked up in jail, she felt as great of a pain as when the two men had pulled the train on her and raped her.

At Halleigh's silence, Mimi continued her reasoning. "It ain't about you, it's about their son. They want him out of there just as much as you do. That's who I would be going to see if I were you." Mimi hopped up off the bed and left the room.

Halleigh tried not to let Mimi's words override her own thoughts on the situation, but she couldn't help it. *It will take me forever to make ten G's by myself. I don't even know what type of job Manolo gon' give me. What if it's only making minimum wage or something? Maybe I should go to Malek's parents and let them know that I can at least pay half of his bail. It will probably be a whole lot easier for me to come up with half of the money rather than all of it. Besides, if they can put up half, we can get Malek out faster. And on top of that, maybe my sacrifice to get the money will finally show Mrs. Johnson how much I love her son. Then she'll finally accept me.*

The next day, Halleigh found herself breathing erratically as she stood on Mrs. Johnson's doorstep. She was nervous, and she knew she looked a mess, but she hoped that Mrs. Johnson would put their beef to the side and agree to help her get Malek out of jail.

I'm just gon' tell her that this is not about us. Her son is sitting downtown in jail, and if we work together, we can get him out. I love him, and so does she. I know she won't just let him sit in there. She has to help me.

At first, when Halleigh asked Mimi to take her to Malek's house, she realized that it was Sunday and that Mrs. Johnson might probably be in church praying for her son to get out of jail. But when they pulled up in front of the house, her car was parked right outside.

Mrs. Johnson had decided against going to church for two reasons. One, the reporters were still outside her doorstep early morning, only vacating the premises when they realized that she wasn't going to answer the door to comment on her son's situation. Secondly, the last thing she wanted was for all those gossiping heifers at her church to pretend to comfort her and pray for her, just so they could have something to talk about. Hell, she might as well have talked to the reporters in that case.

Just as Halleigh was about to knock on the door, she saw Mrs. Johnson look through the curtains. Halleigh thought once she saw her that she would answer the door, but she didn't. *I know she knows I'm out here,* Halleigh thought in frustration. Tired of playing games, she knocked on the door with force. She shouted, "Mrs. Johnson, please open the door. We need to talk!" She heard the bolt lock click.

Mrs. Johnson opened the door with a stone face. "Stop beating on my door," she said, no emotion in her voice. Her eyes were red, and she still wore her house coat, even though it was one o'clock in the afternoon.

Halleigh looked the woman in the eyes. "I'm sorry, but please . . . I need to talk to you."

"What do you want, little girl? Haven't you done enough damage?" Mrs. Johnson said coldly. Her eyes pierced Halleigh's soul like a pair of machetes, her glare was so cold. "You've already ruined my son's life, now what?"

"Listen, I love Malek, and I know you think that I'm a gold-digger and that I'm only with him because he's going to the NBA, but that's not true."

Halleigh could see that Mrs. Johnson was about ready to close the door on her, so she quickly put her cards on the table. "Look, I know you don't like me, but this is not about me. I'm here because I want to help Malek. I know that you and Mr. Johnson work hard just to maintain, and probably don't have money stored away to get him out of jail, and I can't help him by myself. I think I can come up with half of the money for his bail. If you all can put up the other half, we can help him together."

Mrs. Johnson just stared at Halleigh without any expression on her face. Her heart hated the girl that stood before her. In a way she was jealous of the way that Malek felt about Halleigh. For so long it had just been her and her son, until her husband came into her life. And before him, they never had much, but as long as they had each other, it always seemed to be enough. Mr. Johnson did some telemarketing sales work, but was mostly in and out of town with his second job as a Kirby Sweeper salesman, going to different conventions and traveling afar in search of new clients. So even now, it was still pretty much her and Malek in the house. And if Mrs. Johnson was being honest with herself, Mr. Johnson only married her out of guilt from his own childhood.

After meeting Malek and befriending him, and Malek so quickly taking to him as if he were his biological father, Mr. Johnson couldn't imagine exiting the boy's life. So he did what was right and committed himself to the family.

When Malek met Halleigh, Mrs. Johnson had to

share her son's heart, and it hurt her dearly. She felt as if Malek had given up so much just to be with her, and that he didn't even know that the young girls these days were all alike. They come a dime a dozen, and they come running when their so-called man is on top, but are the first to get ghost when things look as though they're about to crumble. That's why Mrs. Johnson was a little surprised herself that Halleigh was trying to stick around, now that her son was obviously at his worst. But even that didn't melt the hard ice around her heart as she looked at Halleigh and thought, *I will never let her get her claws in my son's back again.*

She figured this was the perfect opportunity to get rid of Halleigh and she took it. Mrs. Johnson burst into patronizing laughter right in Halleigh's face. "Sweetheart, do you really think that I would let my son stay in jail? That his father would let him stay in jail? Malek came home this morning," she lied. "Being a future NBA star has its perks."

A smile spread across Halleigh's face. "Can I see him, please?" she asked. "I just want to make sure he's all right."

"Halleigh, I'm sorry to be the one to break this to you, but Malek left this morning. His father came into town and thought that it would be good for him if he got away from all this madness until things died down." Mrs. Johnson was starting to believe the fable herself, and so she continued to add yeast to make it rise. "He didn't want to see you, honey. He said that you were the reason why his chances of getting in the NBA was now jeopardized. He'll be lucky to even get a decent college to accept him after this little stunt."

Tears built up in Halleigh's eyes from the news she had just received. "Mrs. Johnson, can you please just call him? Just let me talk to him?"

"I'm sorry, honey, but he asked me not to give you or anyone else his number, and I have to respect his wishes. I know that you and I have had our days, but I truly am sorry that you had to hear this from me, the same way I had to hear about my son being in jail from you." Mrs. Johnson cleared her throat, forcing down the sarcasm stuck there. "He just feels that it's time to move on with his life. A life that no longer includes you."

On the inside, Mrs. Johnson was smiling, pleased with her deception. She could tell that her words were breaking the young girl's heart into a thousand pieces. *Anything to take care of my baby. He doesn't need her in his life,* she thought.

Mrs. Johnson knew that Malek's arraignment was set for the next morning, but she refused to let Halleigh know that. *I'll do anything to keep this girl away from my son.* Mrs. Johnson banked on her perception about the girl being correct, thinking that by later that night the hoodrat would already be sticking her claws into the next boy.

Halleigh was too shocked to move. She was too shocked to speak, so she just watched in desperation as Mrs. Johnson shut the door in her face. Her heart and mind couldn't quite grasp what Malek's mother had told her. *Why would he do this to me?* she thought as she began the long trek back to the

South Side of town, not having Mimi wait on her. She had thought only positive thoughts. She'd go talk to Mrs. Johnson, and then the two of them would work things out.

Halleigh wasn't surprised that Mr. Johnson would scoop Malek up like that. After all, he'd always been the voice of reason in the home. Of course, he didn't care for Halleigh all that much either, but he didn't dislike her the way Mrs. Johnson did. Halleigh couldn't help thinking that things would have turned out different if she'd gotten to Mr. Johnson earlier.

Halleigh tried to hold her tears inside as she treaded through the city, often stopping just to get her thoughts together. It was like she was in a trance. Before she knew it, light became dark, and confidence became insecurity when she thought about her relationship with Malek. She was so sure that he would never leave her. *He promised me that he would take care of me. What am I going to do without him?*

Feeling like her world had come to an end, Halleigh lost all perspective of her circumstances. Her mind went numb, and she headed back toward the new place that she hoped she would be able to call home.

Chapter Eleven

Two days after witnessing the brutal rape of her own daughter, Sharina had shot up a week's worth of products and was in need of a new fix. Actually, she hadn't noticed that Halleigh was gone until she needed her services again.

She ranted and raved through the house, "Halleigh, where the hell are you?" tossing furniture over as if Halleigh was hiding under them.

In a fit, and with a monkey on her back, she tore the house up, searching under tossed pillows on the sofa, under the bed, and in the closets. She even groveled on the carpet with a straw when she thought she saw a white dash of powder. Unfortunately, it wasn't crank (amphetamine) or crack, but a piece of lint.

"Where the hell is that heifer?" she grumbled, scratching an open sore on her arm. "She know I need her. Much as I done did for her, she better be glad I ain't callin' the law on her. If Flint PD wasn't so crooked, I'd report her underage ass. But, hell, the damn cop would probably fuck her too before they even made it to the station."

After what seemed like hours of destruction for Sharina, she had finally worn herself out. The last place she had searched was the bathroom, removing everything from under the sink and the medicine cabinets, and tearing down towels and washcloths from the racks that held them. Sweaty, funky, and exhausted, she slumped down the wall and onto the floor. She stared at the toilet across from her, feeling like a piece of shit, wanting to just dunk her head in and drown herself.

But all of a sudden, it was as if she was having an epiphany. Her eyes lit up as she crawled over to the toilet. She found a little bit of blow that she'd hidden from her friends a few weeks earlier in the bathroom commode. She'd forgotten all about it until now. "Thank you, God," she cried out. "Thank you, Lord," she added, giving God thanks for the devil's work.

Elated at the discovery of the drugs, Sharina snorted some then shot up the rest. "I can quit any time I want," she murmured to herself as her high settled throughout her body, "but I don't wanna." She smiled. "Shit feels too good."

She slumped, and her eyes closed. "I'm gonna get high forever," were the last words she spoke out loud. But the last words she thought were, *And Halleigh's going to help me to be able to do it.*

Chapter Twelve

Manolo watched Mimi step her skinny legs into a purple thong. Her body was slim, but stacked just right, her ass cheeks filling out voluptuously, causing him to lust after her. He asked her, "Where she go?"

"She went to see the young boy's mama." Mimi studied his facial expression to see if he was upset, but saw no sign of anger in his eyes. "Don't worry, she'll be back," she said, once again studying his facial expressions. "You upset?"

"Nah, I ain't mad. We haven't given her a reason not to want to come back. She doesn't know the deal yet. I still got to break li'l mama in." He thought about how easy it was going to be to get into Halleigh's head.

Tasha walked into the room, strutting as if she belonged on a runway. Her layered hair was held out of her face with a pair of large Chloe glasses, and her manicured feet were covered in red flip-flops. She struggled with the many bags in her hand.

"Did you get what I asked you to?" Manolo asked.

Tasha nodded her head, removing outfit after outfit from large shopping bags. The outfits were all revealing, short mini skirts with low-cut tops, and a pair of matching stilettos for each outfit.

Manolo had sent her on a shopping trip for Halleigh. He had big plans for her; she just didn't know it yet.

Mimi observed some of the items, measuring them. "Yeah, she should be able to fit this stuff." She then frowned. "But you sure she's gon' be down for this? She seem kind of timid to me."

Tasha chimed in, "She's taken a bath and cleaned up, but her clothes still look pretty bad. She gonna be able to work it?" Tasha snapped her fingers with the twitch of her ass.

"I gave her something to wear for now," Mimi told her. "She a'ight."

Manolo, tired of hearing the girls go back and forth over his latest project, and whether he could pull off getting her right where he wanted her, said, "Don't worry about it. I'll handle it." He looked at Tasha. "When I first got a hold of your ass, you was the deacon's daughter. Now you the baddest bitch in Flint." He slapped her on the ass. His dick swelled a bit at the thought of Tasha's sweet pussy, and how he had broken her in.

Although only twenty-three, Tasha knew how to

please a man. She was a freak and had no problem giving Manolo the goods anytime he wanted it. That's one of the reasons why he'd made her the madam of the house. He preferred to have her all to himself and didn't want her working niggas anymore. He wasn't trying to share her pussy.

Tasha thought about Manolo's comment. Halleigh did remind her of herself a little bit when she first got into the game. Which is why a part of her was a little intimidated. She was going to make sure that Halleigh didn't dare try to come after her crown as the queen of that there throne.

Mimi rolled her eyes at both Manolo and Tasha. *Bitch always getting special treatment.* She then finished dressing, looking as Manolo pulled Tasha toward him, grinding his swollen dick into her backside.

All of a sudden, they heard the front door slam. They saw Halleigh run past Manolo's bedroom and into her own. They could hear her crying.

Tasha shook her head and sighed. "You better save that for her." She rubbed Manolo's crotch. "It looks like you gon' have your work cut out for you." She then maneuvered herself out of his grasp and left the room, taking Mimi with her. "We'll be at the hotel," she said, knowing Manolo would want privacy while he entertained the young girl.

Manolo paid for hotel rooms on a weekly basis for his girls to turn their tricks. This way he could more easily keep an eye on them and their johns. On a regular basis, he would show up there unannounced, so the girls had to be on their toes at all times.

Manolo wore some sea-green slacks with matching gators, and a white wife-beater that showed his tattooed arms. He had a button-up shirt to match the slacks, but it was thrown across the chair in his room. He walked into the hallway and knocked lightly on the frame of Halleigh's door, announcing his presence, even though the door was already ajar. He walked inside over to where Halleigh lay across the bed sobbing.

Halleigh was on the floor crying so hard, she didn't even notice he was standing beside her.

"You a'ight?" he asked in his well-rehearsed tone of fake concern.

Halleigh quickly tried to brush her tears away, turning her head toward the wall and away from Manolo. "Yeah, I'm good," she replied. Her voice cracked in mid-sentence. She broke down in sobs at the thought of all of the words Mrs. Johnson had said to her earlier that day.

Manolo sat down next to her. He put his hand on her back and guided her head into his lap. He then gently began to rub her head, massaging her neck as he listened to her cry. "Shhh, tell Nolo what's wrong, baby girl," he whispered. He blew air into her ear in a seemingly innocent way.

Halleigh couldn't respond. Every time she attempted to speak, her words got caught in her throat, and she found herself weeping even harder.

"Don't talk, baby," Manolo said, trying to soothe her. "Just get it all out."

Halleigh cried and cried until she felt emptied out. She eventually stopped crying but still couldn't speak. Her eyes burned as she stared blankly at the wall.

Afterwards, Manolo and Halleigh sat in silence in the same spot for an hour. He asked her, "So are you ready to talk yet?"

Halleigh sniffed. "He left me," she said, her voice cracking again. "You were right. He blamed me for getting arrested, and he left me." Just hearing herself say it made more tears spill down Halleigh's face.

"It's okay, baby girl. You'll be okay."

"He was all I had," she said, her voice breaking up from the thought of being alone in the world.

Manolo could hear the pain in her voice, a pain that put a devious smile on his insides. But he had to stay in character. He eased her head down in his lap and massaged her scalp and her hair. He kept smoothing back her hair. "You've got me, baby girl. Fuck that nigga. He just up and left you. He don't know how to hold you down. I bet he promised he would always take care of you, huh?"

Just like clockwork, Halleigh nodded.

"And now when you need him most, he gets ghost on you." Manolo paused. "And besides, he let somebody else touch you, baby girl. If he was really your man, he would've handled that for you. Fuck robbing a store with a bottle. He should have been shoving that bottle up the mu'fuckas' asses who did that shit to you."

Manolo spoke in a low, hypnotic voice. He slowly ran his hands all over Halleigh's body, sending chills up her spine. Suddenly tears flooded Halleigh's vision. She had a flashback as to how powerless she felt when she was being raped and began to shake uncontrollably.

He lifted her head out of his lap and looked into her eyes. "They hurt you, didn't they?"

She nodded her head and dropped it shamefully into her chest.

"It makes me crazy just thinking about somebody hurting someone as sweet and innocent as you. That nigga should've protected you."

Halleigh gazed up in surprise at how upset Manolo had become.

"Fuck that, Halleigh," he continued, going for the Oscar nomination at least. "Any nigga put his hands on you, they gotta die." He stood up and motioned for Halleigh to follow him into his bedroom, where he pulled a .45 out of his closet.

Halleigh's eyes bucked at the sight of the pistol. She put her hands up to calm Manolo down. "No, wait a minute," she said. "I don't even know who did it. I don't know who they are."

The way he had erupted in anger scared her, but excited her at the same time. Her mother didn't protect her, Malek didn't protect her, but here someone who had barely known her was willing to protect her. Willing to make sure that the two bastards who had raped her never had the opportunity to touch her again.

"Fuck! If you don't know the cats who did this to you, then I'm going for the next best thing—that nigga Malek. That mu'fucka should've held you down, Halleigh. Fuck basketball and the NBA. You was supposed to be his girl. I'm murking that stupid nigga for letting them get away with it," he yelled, inserting the clip and pulling back the chamber of the gun.

"No!" Halleigh yelled as she rushed to Manolo to grab the pistol from his hand. "No, don't!" She couldn't even fathom the thought of Manolo harming Malek. She especially didn't want to be the cause of it. She had already been the cause of enough bad luck in Malek's life. She removed the gun from Manolo's hands.

He closed his eyes and wrapped his arms around her waist. "I'm sorry, baby girl. I'm sorry if I scared you. I just want to keep you safe, baby girl, that's all." His voice took on a syrupy tone. He held on to her tight. "I want you to feel safe," he repeated, as if he had known her all his life and it was his duty to keep her secure.

Halleigh held on tightly to Manolo. The truth was, he did make her feel safe. The fact that he wanted revenge on the dudes who'd hurt her made her feel special. Like he truly cared for her.

"He doesn't love you. He wasn't treating you right, Halleigh," he whispered in her ear and then kissed it.

For a moment, his touch reminded her of Malek's. And for a moment, she closed her eyes and envisioned that it was Malek's touch.

"He promised you all that, but he left you here in Flint while he's living it up without you."

Once again, Manolo was right. Why was she

shedding tears over Malek when he had picked up and left her for dead? "Why did he do this to me?" she asked him in dismay.

"Because he doesn't know what he had," Manolo told her. "He don't deserve you." As he continued to speak, he could feel Halleigh dropping her guards. Her body loosened up as he held on to her, and she began to breathe heavily as she, too, brought her body closer to his.

Her broken heart had left her vulnerable to Manolo's manipulation. Her broken heart, as well as being thrown away and discarded by everybody who she felt should have loved and protected her and didn't—her father, her mother, and now Malek. She needed to hear the words that Manolo was speaking. She needed to know that there was still one person in the world who hadn't thrown her away, even if it was a damn-near stranger. Every girl needed to be loved and to feel the way that he was making her feel. Any emotion felt better than the pain that everyone else had caused her. Any direction was better than being lost, and being wanted by somebody, anybody, was better than being discarded by everyone. How could she turn down Manolo's offer of protection?

"Let me take care of you, baby girl," he whispered, bringing his lips from her ear to her lips. Only inches away from her face, he was holding her so tight, not wanting her to have the option of backing away from him. "Nobody wants you, baby. Nobody loves you. But I see something in you. I want you. Can I make you mine?" He put his finger under her chin then kissed the tears rolling down her face.

Halleigh nodded her head as Manolo moved in to kiss her softly on the lips. She was hesitant at first, but he kissed her so deeply that she convinced herself that he was being sincere.

Manolo's kisses made their way from her lips to her breasts, to her stomach, and finally to her belt buckle, where he lingered, while her hands rested on his neatly waved taper.

"Baby girl, I want you. Do you belong to me?" he asked her. He unzipped the loose-fitting Baby Phat pants that she'd borrowed from Mimi. When she didn't respond, he said, "Tell me that you're mine, baby girl." He softly pushed Halleigh back on the bed, and with the precision of a heart surgeon, pulled her panties off.

She gasped as her heart beat uncontrollably. *What is he doing to me?* she thought.

"Tell me," he repeated.

He parted her legs, and let his tongue roll softly over her throbbing clitoris. She was still hesitant. He could tell that she was holding back, but when he inserted two fingers into her vagina, he knew she was willing. *I've just got to get her to say it,* he thought. *I've got to make her think my feelings for her are real.* He caressed her thick thighs and plump ass as he buried his tongue into her pussy. He lifted her hips up and fucked her with his tongue.

"Hmm," she moaned. She began to grind her hips

on his face, gripping his processed hair and holding on for dear life. "Hmm, hmm," she moaned as he went to work.

"Tell me, who's Daddy? Who do you belong to?" he asked between licks.

"I'm yours," she moaned, moving her hips in circle eights, as if she was at a rodeo. "I belong to you."

"Who am I? What's my name?" he demanded. "Whose are you?"

"I'm yours, Daddy."

"Whose pussy is this?" he asked. He knew he was the man when it came to eating pussy. His head game was fierce, so he knew what her answer would be, even before she moaned back her response.

"Yours, Nolo. I'm yours, Daddy."

Got her. He positioned her in the middle of the bed, spread her legs even farther apart, and put his body on top of hers. His manhood stood at attention, her seventeen-year-old body drawing him to her like a magnet to steel. He couldn't wait to enter her. He groped her blossoming titties and took her dark nipples into his mouth.

Halleigh looked down at what she was inviting between her legs, fear gripping her as she thought about how badly it hurt when Riq had entered her walls for the very first time, busting through her like a football team would a banner on homecoming night.

Manolo felt her body tense up, and saw tears resurface on her face. He licked her face, wiping the tears away with his hot tongue like a mother cat cleans her kittens. "What them niggas did to you don't count," he said, knowing exactly what to say to make her feel better. "Baby girl, *this* is your first time, and I'm going to make it right for you. I'm not going to hurt you."

She didn't say another word, relaxing her legs to allow him to enter her easily. Pain was what hit her first as his thick nine inches eased into her. She felt like her insides were once again being ripped out of her. She arched her back and tried to scoot her body away from him.

"Relax," he whispered as he began to pump in and out of her in a slow rhythm, as if he was moving to a silent melody.

Halleigh closed her eyes and dug her nails into his back, moving her hips in unison with his, as pain transformed into pleasure.

She didn't know it yet, but by giving her body to Manolo first, she was also giving him her head. She, like most women, equated love with sex. It wasn't going to be hard for Manolo to have his way with her, to create and control her little world.

Afterwards, her body was sore as she lay beside Manolo. She was quiet because she didn't know what to say. She hoped that it was good enough for him to want to keep her around. She knew that this was probably the reason all the other girls got to stay around. She had nowhere else to go, so if this is what it took, so be it. He'd promised to keep her safe, and she believed he would make good on his promise, unlike all the other liars in her life.

121

"Are you sore?" he asked her as he held her from behind.

"A little bit," she answered in a low voice. Her mind drifted back to Malek. *Why did he leave me?* she thought.

I got to get the kid off her mind. Manolo asked, "What's on your mind?" already knowing the answer to his question.

"Nothing."

He sat up and pulled her into his lap, and she sat between his legs, her back against his chest and her head resting on his shoulder.

"Look, Halleigh," he stated firmly, "I know what you been through, and I know you've got feelings for ol' boy. But I got to be honest with you. I can't be involved with no bitch—excuse me, baby girl. I don't need to refer to you like that, because you are anything but that. But when I think of you having feelings for another dude, I just get..." His words trailed off, and then he continued without finishing his original thought. "Point is, if you gon' be here with me, you've got to be loyal. Loyalty is important. If I can't trust you, I don't want you. Now, I'm not trying to do you like everybody else in your life and leave you, but I need to know this now before I get all caught up in you and end up being hurt by you leaving me."

Quickly, she responded like Tina Turner in the movie *What's Love Got to Do with It,* "I would never leave you." Halleigh knew what it felt like to be walked out on by her own blood, by people who she thought would be there to take care of her.

She wasn't about to do that same thing to someone else and walk out on them. *Never*, she thought.

"I just need to know who you gon' ride for?" he asked.

"You," she replied without hesitation.

"Are you sure?" He turned her chin so he could see into her eyes. "Because if I see you or even hear about you messing with another nigga, especially that nigga you *was* fucking with, I'm-a kill 'em, you dig?"

"I understand," she replied. Her thoughts kept finding their way back to Malek, but he had hurt her beyond forgiveness. She knew that Manolo would never hurt her.

"So tell me who Daddy is, my little Sunshine." He tongue-kissed her sloppily on the lips.

"You are. You're Daddy," she responded with a grateful smile, happy that for the first time in her life she had a "daddy."

Chapter Thirteen

Jamaica Joe and his attorney strolled out of the police precinct toward a white Bentley parked right out front. Joe's head henchman, Tariq, was sitting on the hood, waiting for his boss.

Once Joe reached the bottom of the steps, he said to his attorney, "Thanks for coming so quickly. Those mu'fuckas fuck with me any chance they get." Joe was still upset about the Flint police and the petty traffic stop they'd made that led to his arrest.

"No problem, Joe." Wallace flashed a slight grin. "That's what you pay me for."

Joe looked over at Tariq and nodded his head. Tariq immediately went into his all-black hoody and pulled out a wad of money in a rubber band. He tossed it to Wallace, making it land right in the palm of his hands.

"Have a nice night, gentlemen," Wallace said.

He shook Joe's hand then turned and headed to his own Bentley.

"Let's get the fuck outta here, fam," Joe said as he slid into the passenger side of his own car.

Tariq jumped into the driver's side and pulled off. He began to put Joe up on the latest. "Yo, you know that nigga Sweets is talking big shit about the Berston Park Battle. I heard he even recruited some NBA players to play on his team this year," Tariq said, referring to the basketball game that was held every year at Berston Park.

"Oh yeah?" Joe's interest was piqued, although he tried to act indifferent.

It was the only time that Joe and Sweets would be in the same vicinity and not trying to kill each other. It was like an unspoken oath to the city—no violence at the Berston Park Battle. Berston Park was like a sacred ground to the city, and both sides respected it.

Joe and Sweets had been enemies for years and had a mutual hatred toward each other. Both of them wanted control of the city's drug trade and were standing in each other's way. Joe ran the North Side of Flint, and Sweets ran the South Side. Once a year, they sponsored a basketball team for the Berston game, and their teams battled it out on the court. For the last four years, Sweets had been victorious, enabling him to carry bragging rights over from one year to the next. Plus any money that was put up on the game.

Very few people knew that Jamaica Joe had come from a middle-class Christian family in Fayetteville,

North Carolina. His father used to be a principal, and his mother, a school teacher. Every one of his three sisters had graduated from college. Jamaica Joe, the youngest in the family, was an only son. From the time he was born, he was spoiled rotten to the bone. But it wasn't his upbringing that had made him a drug kingpin. It was just something in his blood. He loved the streets from the time he was a teenager.

After doing a one-year stint for armed robbery in a juvenile camp, he was released at the age of eighteen and moved to Flint. He'd heard the drug trade was really jumping off there. He'd now been living there for the past twenty years in relative wealth and wielded some power.

Joe was noticeably bothered by the mention of Sweet's name. "Fuck that faggot-ass mu'fucka," he said. He searched through his phone to see what messages he'd received while locked up. He continued, "Send word to his crew that I'm willing to put up fifty thousand, winner take all."

"I'll put the news out in the streets," Tariq said, maneuvering the luxury car through downtown Flint.

Joe suddenly thought about Malek. The Latino man in the jail cell might not have known who Malek was, but he did. He knew Malek's skills; that he was an NBA prospect. *I need that nigga on my squad. Li'l man got heart.* He remembered how Malek held his own in the bullpen. *I know that young cat got some street-ball skills in him too.*

Joe was very familiar with Malek's ball game. He

frequently gambled on Malek's high school games, and whether Malek knew it or not, he'd made Joe a lot of money through his phenomenal plays. He pulled out his cell and dialed Wallace's number. "Yo, I need a favor," he said as he laid back in his seat.

Chapter Fourteen

Attorney Wallace stood next to Malek before Judge William Kennedy. "Your Honor," he said, "we move to have the case dismissed due to lack of evidence."

It was Monday morning, and the first case on Judge Kennedy's docket. The courtroom was filled to capacity with press, cameras, news reporters, and spectators, and the judge had to call the court to order more than once.

Loyal fans just couldn't bring themselves to believe that someone with such a bright future ahead of them would throw it all away like that. They kept chanting, "Free Malek, free Malek, free Malek," only stopping their chants when the judge threatened to close the courtroom and put everybody out.

Wallace continued, "Your Honor, I submit that

Malek Johnson has been the victim of the most heinous form of racism. This young man has no priors, is a model student, and is the number one national prospect for the NBA. For the life of me, I don't understand how Mr. Chiu could slander my client like this. This has to be a miscarriage of justice."

Malek's mother sat on the front row, her lip trembling, tears glazing her eyes, and his stepfather sat next to her. Mrs. Johnson had kept her promise to her son by not calling her husband to inform him about Malek's arrest. She'd hoped and prayed that her son would be free from jail and at home before his father found out. That way things wouldn't have seemed so bad. But after seeing footage of his son on ESPN, Mr. Johnson made a beeline home.

Malek couldn't believe how Anderson Wallace shredded the prosecution to pieces, making it seem like he'd done no wrong. Wallace even produced an eyewitness who claimed to have seen the whole ordeal. The witness, a retired cop to boot, testified that he was taking his regular jog, when the streets were quiet and clear, and saw with his very own eyes Malek get racially profiled and discriminated against by the Asian storeowner. He testified how Malek had just been walking by when, out of nowhere, the storeowner came running from the store and pointed him out as the man who'd just robbed his store.

"Any black man walking by would have been accused of the robbery that night," the witness said in an ever so convincing tone. "Hell, it could have been me." He claimed that the overzealous store-owner jumped the gun.

Anderson Wallace flipped the script and made Malek look like the victim, rather than the criminal. That's why Wallace was the best.

Malek didn't understand how this attorney had come to his parents and volunteered to defend him for free. It had only been two days since the botched robbery, and already he was on the verge of having his image being restored.

The DA's office was too worried about Anderson Wallace filing a civil suit against them and just wanted to end the case as soon as possible. The prosecuting attorney, Jack Byrne, stood up and cleared his throat. He said, "Uhh, Your Honor, uhh, we too request that the case be dismissed."

Wallace looked over at the prosecution and smiled as he relished in another victory. Fifty-two wins and no losses, to be exact.

The judge looked at Byrne skeptically. "Are you sure?"

"Yes, sir, we're quite sure," the prosecutor affirmed.

The judge bellowed in a stentorian voice, "Case dismissed!" and banged his gavel resolutely.

Malek smiled and looked back at his mother and his father with relief and joy. His father held his fist up and shook it in victory, as if to say, "The truth will always prevail. I knew my boy wasn't capable of making such a stupid decision." Malek then looked at his mother, who knew the truth, but had kept her word in not telling his father what had really gone down, that he really did hold up the convenient store. It was their secret.

Malek noticed too that his agent/adviser was sitting in the courtroom. He had a look on his face as if, all of a sudden, a Good Samaritan had just returned the suitcase with a million dollars that someone had stolen. He was cheering louder for Malek than he ever had at one of his basketball games.

As Wallace guided Malek and his parents out of the courtroom, Malek then turned back to Wallace and gratefully shook his hand. As soon as they opened the double doors, cameras flashed away. ESPN reporters were frantically trying to get a comment from the newly acquitted NBA prospect.

Malek's agent acted as security, helping his client through the massive crowd. "No comment, no comment."

Once they reached the front steps of the courthouse Malek looked at Wallace. "I don't know who you are, but thank you." He breathed a sigh of relief.

"Yes, thank you," Mr. Johnson said, shaking Wallace's hand nonstop. "Thank you for getting the truth out about my boy." He turned to his wife and son. "You two, wait here. I'm going to go ahead and pull the car around."

"Thank you, honey." Mrs. Johnson watched her husband walk off to go retrieve their car. She then turned to Wallace. "Like my husband, I can't thank you enough for what you did for our son. But I do make one heck of a pineapple upside down cake." She smiled.

"You are all quite welcome," Wallace said, "but I'm not the one you should be thanking." He motioned his head to a tinted Bentley parked across the street. Malek was confused. He was relieved to be out of jail and having his case dismissed completely, but he still was confounded as to how he got off. He wanted to see who was responsible for his miraculous exoneration. "I'll be right back." He kissed his mother and shook his agent's hand before jogging across the street to the car, where a young man with an iced-out chain and long braids was sitting on the hood.

Once he reached the car, Tariq acknowledged him, slowly throwing his head up. "What up?"

Malek nodded his head in response.

Before Tariq could say anything else, the back window of the car slowly rolled down, and Jamaica Joe's face emerged. "Get in," he said as he hit the unlock button.

Malek turned and looked at his mother, who was standing on the steps and chatting with his agent as she waited for his father. "Ma," he shouted. When he got her attention, he said, "You and Dad go ahead home. I'll catch up with you in a minute."

Mrs. Johnson wanted to disagree, fearing he might be going to try to see that hoodrat girlfriend of his. He hadn't even noticed yet that she wasn't there to support him. But Malek had already climbed into Joe's car before she could say anything.

Tariq also got in the car and looked at Joe through the rearview.

"Wanna take a ride?" Joe asked Malek.

"Cool."

As the reporters circled the car, trying to take pictures through the tinted glass, Joe nodded his head, and Tariq pulled away from the chaos.

Malek had heard a lot about Jamaica Joe, most of which was bad. He couldn't understand why Joe had helped him out. The first thing on his mind was extortion. *This nigga must gon' try to ask for ten times more when I get drafted.* Malek looked around at the soft leather interior and then at Joe's presidential Rolex. *The way things look, I know he ain't hurting for cash.* "Thanks for having your lawyer on my case. He saved me, for real."

"No doubt," Joe replied. "You're young, black, and talented. Them white folks would love to keep you down." He lit a blunt and let the smoke curl out the corner of his mouth.

"What's the catch?" Malek asked, trying to get straight to the point.

"See, that's what's wrong with our people. We don't believe in helping our own out without expecting something in return. How do you know I'm not just lending a helping hand?"

"Because ain't shit in this world free."

"You a smart man. That's why I like you." Joe took another puff of his blunt. "Li'l nigga smart." He tossed the comment at Tariq as though Malek wasn't present. "This weekend my team is playing in the annual Berston charity game. I would appreciate if you would play on my squad."

Malek remained silent for a second. He knew about the tournament. It was the biggest event of the year, and he always went to watch it. He wanted to play in it, but after his popularity soared, his agent advised him not to play in non-school athletics to avoid getting injured.

"I don't know. My agent—"

"You a man, right?" Joe said calmly.

"No doubt." Malek lifted his chin and puffed out his chest.

"Stand on ya own two. Take your balls out your socks. It's just a one-day tournament. You gon' let some agent punk you?"

Malek pondered his situation for a moment. First, he took into consideration Joe's act of kindness. He knew that if it wasn't for Joe, he would be in jail facing robbery charges. After all, what was one game?

"I'll play," he said, evenly, and without flinching.

Chapter Fifteen

Manolo sexed Halleigh crazy for a week in celebration of her eighteenth birthday, breaking her in, teaching her how to drive a nigga crazy with her body. He showed her how to do the Kegel exercises, sticking his finger inside of her and having her tighten up a hundred times, to keep her vaginal muscles taut. He taught her how to suck dick, how to take it from the back, and how to be seductive without being trashy.

She didn't know she was being groomed for every other man in the world. She just thought she was being groomed for Manolo. After all, he had expressed his anger at just the thought of her being with another man. So why would she think he would be training her to do just that?

During that first week, Manolo showed all the concern of a loving man. He sent Halleigh to Planned Parenthood to make sure she hadn't caught a disease from the train the two men pulled on her. Even when the clinic said she didn't have any infections or anything, Manolo gave her some of Mimi's STD antibiotics to take for a week. Next, he gave her the morning-after pills until her period came.

After she had her menstrual cycle, Manolo sat her on the side of the bath tub and showed her how to take a douche. "That's just to clean out all the toxins," he told her.

He also showed her how to properly wash her body after having sex with him. "Front to the back," he would say, pointing to her vaginal area. "I like clean women."

As a precaution, he also put Halleigh on birth control pills. Manolo became like the mother she sorely missed, providing her with the things a mother would, to usher her into young womanhood; right down to teaching her how to use a tampon properly. Before she only used Maxi pads.

But even while on her period she had to make money, so he had to show her how to plug it up and take care of business without a trick knowing she was on the rag. Some niggas didn't care. They were grimy like that. But some were disgusted by just the thought of a woman having the curse.

All along, Halleigh thought that he was teaching her how he wanted his woman to be. She didn't think twice about the freaky things he did to her. She couldn't tell him no. Even though she knew that she wasn't his only girl, she felt like they had a connection.

As the days passed, she became aware that Manolo was somewhat of a pimp. That all the girls weren't just for his selfish pleasures, even though he didn't mind helping himself if the price was right. She noticed how the other women sashayed around naked, or wearing only boa feathers around their necks, but at dinner time, whenever everyone was present, they sat down and ate like one big, happy family.

In return for offering his place to his girls, they worked for him out of the Best Western, trading sexual favors for cash. He also was part-owner of a strip club called Wild Thangs, where some of his girls worked for extra ducats.

His profession and what he did with the other girls didn't bother Halleigh though, as long as he kept his promise to her. She was too far-gone on Manolo's loving to care.

She was so enthralled with Manolo, she figured that she was just as important to him as Tasha appeared to be. They were the only two girls in the house that he never put to work, and she loved the attention. She had no idea that pretty soon, she would be old news and would have to pay later for all of the things he was doing for her now.

Halleigh stared at herself in the mirror as Tasha stood behind her and flat-ironed her shoulder-length hair. She wore light denim Deron shorts. Her white and gold halter top revealed her newly pierced navel. The MAC cosmetics that Tasha applied to her face gave her a mature look instead of the schoolgirl look.

Halleigh liked the change in appearance. She had never been more secure in herself in her entire life; the sexier style giving her a boost in confidence.

"Y'all ready?" Manolo asked. He stepped into the room. He examined Mimi, Halleigh, and Tasha from head to toe. His eyes lingered on Halleigh. Her denim shorts were so short, you could see where her ass cheeks darkened. Manolo licked his lips at the voluptuous sight. *This bitch gon' make me some money.*

This would be the first time Manolo put Halleigh to work. He knew that the Berston Park annual game was the perfect place for her to make her debut. Niggas from all over Flint, and even major players from Detroit, would be in attendance, all looking for pussy. Dollars would flow like wine from a vineyard, and Manolo made sure that his bitches would be there to drink it up.

"Yeah, we almost ready, Nolo." Tasha watched through the mirror as he approached Halleigh. *I hope she's ready.* She was aware of Halleigh's illusions that Manolo loved her and didn't even want her looking at another man. *Wait until she finds out that not only he don't give a damn if another man looks at her, but that he wants her to fuck them.* She chuckled to herself as she tossed on more makeup.

"You look good, Sunshine," Manolo whispered to Halleigh.

Halleigh blushed. She loved when Manolo called

her Sunshine. It literally brightened her mood. She lowered her head and replied in a low tone, "Thanks."

"You know it's gon' be a lot of niggas there trying to step to you—"

Halleigh interrupted him. "You don't have to worry 'bout that. I'm with you."

"Nah, baby girl. Niggas gon' be tryin'-a see you. Put your game down and do you. It's time for you to make Daddy proud."

A look of confusion flashed across Halleigh's face.

He could see the reluctance in her eyes as she realized what he was trying to say. "You with me? You down for Daddy, right?"

She nodded.

"Then it's time for you to make me a proud poppa." He turned her toward him by her shoulders. "Look, I done showed you how a nigga like to be treated. Now I need you to use what I taught you and make it work for you. Bring Daddy that paper," he said, kissing her on the neck.

Halleigh just stood there like a frozen popsicle. Was she really hearing what she was hearing? He kissed her on the cheek and then stroked her cheek with the back of his hand, sending sensual chills through her body.

He leaned into her ear. "You're not Daddy's little girl anymore," he whispered, his lips lightly brushing up against her ear. "It's time to grow up and earn your keep; earn your spot in this house and in my life."

The last thing Halleigh wanted was to lose her place in Manolo's heart, not to mention a bed to sleep in at night. She thought about how alone, cold, and afraid she was the night of the rape. Then Mimi took her out of the rain and home to Manolo. They were all her family now, and she never wanted to be out on the streets alone and cold again. With that thought, Halleigh nodded her head in agreement. She was so lost, she didn't even second-guess what Manolo was asking her to do. How could she tell him no after all that he had done for her? She didn't see that she was being used. She only saw that Manolo wanted her, which was more than she could say about anyone else in her life.

Manolo, Tasha, and Mimi left the room, Halleigh trailing slowly behind them. They all got into an old-school Monte Carlo. It was sitting on "grown man's" and had a fresh money-green paint job. Manolo got into the car.

Before the girls entered, Tasha turned around and whispered to Mimi and Halleigh, "Sweets gon' be there, so make sure y'all are about that paper today. If a nigga ain't talking money, keep it pushing."

Mimi didn't respond. She already knew what was up. Although Manolo took care of them, and he was the one they were indebted to, he reported to Sweets.

Sweets had the South Side of Flint on smash and had a notorious reputation in the hood. With Sweets behind him, Manolo was able to keep the sex game on lock, recruiting the baddest bitches in town. And as long as he split his profits with Sweets, he had the muscle he needed to run his business however he pleased. Sweets respected Manolo's hustle so much, he even went in on a strip joint with him.

Mimi knew that whenever Sweets was around, she had to be about her money if she didn't want his foot in her ass.

Halleigh nodded her head, and Tasha got on into the car. Before Halleigh got in, she grabbed Mimi's arm and quietly asked, "Who's Sweets?"

With a matter-of-fact look on her face, Mimi replied, "You don't want to know."

Chapter Sixteen

Berston Park was packed for the first day of the big game. The sun was shining brightly, and the sky was a clear blue with no signs of clouds anywhere on the horizon. Both young and old were present. Flint families were happy to bring their children out to a decent outing, and they all eagerly anticipated a good game. They'd heard that Malek, the number one high school prospect, would be playing. Some of the top gamblers in town had a lot riding on the game. The odds were 2-1 in favor of Sweets' team, since he'd won the past few years.

The excited onlookers in the bleachers kept cheering, "Malek! Malek! Malek!"

Malek warmed up for the game by dribbling the ball on the court, his eyes all the while scanning the crowd in search of Halleigh. He had desperately searched for her in spite of his mother telling him that she had showed up on their doorstep confessing that she had ruined his life and had decided to break up with him.

"I told you that little tramp only wanted you for your money," Mrs. Johnson told Malek. "Now that the chips are down and she thinks you don't have a chance in the world at the NBA, she's left you hanging."

That statement was only confirmed after Malek realized and thought about the fact that Halleigh hadn't bothered to show up for his court date.

It was hard for Malek to believe that Halleigh had left him hanging. He had even gone to her mother's home looking for her, just so that he could hear it coming straight from her mouth that she didn't want to be with him anymore. But he arrived only to find drug junkies scattered throughout the living room, and no sign of Halleigh.

"Miss Walters, have you seen Halleigh?" he asked Sharina.

"No. I don't know where that heifer is," her mother said, scratching her pus-cratered arms. "I thought she was with you."

"You mean she hasn't been home?"

"No. But if you see that li'l bitch, tell her to get her ass home. I got things for her to do."

He smirked. *Yeah, right. Like being your little trick?*

Malek really was beginning to get worried as the days passed. Where could she have gone off to if she didn't go back home? She didn't have anybody else. And Nikki hadn't seen her since the night of the championship game.

Malek shook his thoughts about Halleigh and tried to focus on the game that was about to take place. As both teams filled the court and the game was about to start, all eyes were on him. Malek's sports agent had begged him not to play in the game, but Malek believed that he owed Joe this one favor. So being very big on loyalty, he kept his word to Joe and played in the game.

Jamaica Joe stood in the middle of his team wearing a white Sean Jean polo shirt and a crisp pair of Air Force Ones. Sweets emerged from the limo with a Sean John wife-beater, crisp jeans, and new Timberlands, his tattooed body on display and his ripped body shining.

Looking at Sweets, one would never know he was homosexual. Actually, he was bisexual. He slept with both men and women. The ladies lusted after him, but he had no desire to have a relationship with them unless they were moving dope for him. Sweets was a bonafide hustler and ran the South Side single-handedly.

Everyone, from pro athletes to rappers to street legends, was in attendance at the park. Every year the same two teams made it to the championship game: Joe's versus Sweets', north versus south. Every year it was an all-out battle, and the entire city was there to see who would come out victorious.

Sweets took his place on the bench as his players scurried over next to him. He then took a quick glance over at Jamaica Joe, who now waited with his team under a tent across the park. He hated

Joe with a passion, and even though they had an unspoken pact not to war at Berston, he still took every precaution.

His young hit squad was scattered throughout the park, each one carrying twin pistols. They called themselves the Shottah Boyz. The Shottah Boyz were four young killers who Sweets had practically raised, since their mothers were on crack. They all were between the ages of sixteen and twenty-two. Although young, they had a notorious reputation. It was rumored that between the four of them, they had fifty murders under their belt. Rah-Rah was reported to be the craziest. They said at seventeen, he was a stone-cold killer.

The announcer announced that the game was about to start, and the two teams filed back onto the court.

Joe's team huddled around him as he gave them a pep talk. "Let's bring the trophy back to the north. Fuck them niggas! Show 'em how we get down. Bring the title back to the hood."

Joe stuck his fist out, and the whole team put their fist on top of his and yelled, "North Side," in unison.

The game started, and immediately Malek began to take over the game. He had the whole crowd in awe as he played like a man among boys. Even the NBA players on Sweets' team had a problem stopping Malek. They may have been professionals, but Malek was at home, playing on that very same court practically all his life.

Joe sat on the bench watching his team blowout

Sweet's. He couldn't believe how Malek took over the game and single-handedly made Sweet's team look bad. "Yeah, baby!" He clapped loudly, grinning and looking over at Sweets, who was obviously irritated. *Today is a good day, baby. It's gon' be easy taking that faggot mu'fucka's money,* Joe thought as he re-focused his attention on the game.

Meanwhile, Manolo's focus was on how much money his bitches was gon' clock today.

"Damn, look at all this money," Mimi said as the car pulled up to the park. She peeped the massive crowd that had occupied Berston Field House. "It's packed."

Tasha and Manolo stepped out first, and Mimi and Halleigh trailed behind them. Dudes with iced-out neck pieces, and chicks with ass and titties hanging out were all that could be seen. The fact that north and south were in the same place at one time had everyone on edge, so everybody was clicked up.

Mimi and Halleigh went their own way as they split up from Tasha and Manolo. It was so crowded in the small space that Halleigh and Mimi couldn't even see the players on the court.

"Yo, ma, where you going?" a dude asked Halleigh as she walked by him. He was standing with his arms folded across his chest; a white bath towel draped over his head to shield his face from the hot sun. The guy and all of his friends watched her backside; the natural sway of her hips commanding their attention.

Halleigh smiled as she continued to maneuver her way past them.

Mimi stopped in mid-step, causing Halleigh to bump into her. Mimi looked at her like she was crazy.

"What?" Halleigh asked.

"Girl, you better go back over there and make that money." Mimi glanced back at the group of dudes. "I'm trying to get down too. Them niggas is crazy paid. So go on and hook it up." Mimi gave her a light shove.

Halleigh strutted back over to the group of dudes. She stammered to the guy that had called out to her, "Y-y-you, uhh, checking for me?" She tried to look confident, placing her hand on her hip and tilting her head to the side.

He grabbed her hand and held it above her head, commanding her to walk in a full circle while he peeped her up and down. Her juicy ass cheeks shifted from side to side as she turned around. "What's your name, ma?" he asked.

Before Halleigh could respond, Mimi cut in, "What's your government? You all into my girl's shit. How about you let her know who you are and what you're about, then she'll decide if you worth fucking with."

Mimi was arrogant and smart-mouthed, but her looks allowed her to be. The dude smiled and rubbed his goatee as he looked at the two young girls that stood in front of him. He figured they had to be only seventeen or eighteen. He was twenty-six and loved young pussy. "Chill, shorty. I'm Mitch," he said.

Mimi arched her eyebrows. "Well, what's up? What *you* working with?"

"Damn! What are you, her pimp or something?

Can I kick it to your girl for a minute?" he asked politely, but obviously irritated.

"Do you, baby. All I'm saying is, time is money, ya feel me?" Mimi rubbed her fingers together as if she was flipping through bills.

"For real? Y'all getting down like that? You mean all I got to do is pay for this pussy?" He stared at Halleigh in disbelief.

Mimi nudged her.

Meantime, Halleigh's heart was beating out of her chest. "That's all it takes," she said in an embarrassed whisper.

"Shit. Take a walk with me then, shorty." He grabbed Halleigh's hand.

Before she walked away Mimi grabbed her hand and whispered, "Get the money first. Make sure he uses a condom too."

Halleigh nodded, and then she followed him to an '07 Cadillac DeVille.

He opened the door for her. "Get in," he stated.

"You got the cash?" she asked nervously. She looked over her shoulder and looked around. Somehow Mimi's aggressiveness made her feel better. She wished Mimi had followed behind them or something.

"How much you taxing?" he asked. He couldn't believe that the gorgeous young girl in front of him was tricking. She really looked innocent and clean-cut.

How much am I supposed to charge this nigga? she thought. That was the one thing she hadn't been schooled on.

"Two fifty," she said, hoping that she wasn't short-changing herself.

He pulled out three hundred-dollar bills and handed it to her.

As she nestled into the back seat of the car, she felt her chest heave up and down as the small space became hot. Her hands began to sweat when she felt Mitch put his tongue on her neck.

"Come here, ma. Why you all over there?" he asked, pulling out his manhood.

Halleigh psyched herself up. *Just do it. Close your eyes and do what you got to do.* She unbuttoned her shorts and eased out of them. *I'm doing this for Manolo. I'm going to make Daddy proud.* She straddled him and grinded her hips as he touched her breasts, squeezing them a little bit too hard. He slid her thong to the side, pulled out a condom, and slid it on to his throbbing dick.

Halleigh looked down at it. He was a decent size. In fact, he wasn't any bigger than Manolo, and she was grateful because she didn't want it to hurt. She felt as if she was selling her soul to the devil when he put himself inside of her.

When he felt her tight walls, he said, "Shit! Ma, you a virgin?"

She gripped him. From the way he moaned she could tell that he loved the way the inside of her felt. At the same time, a tear fell from her eyes as she stared out of the rear windshield and rode his dick.

"Damn, ma, you working it. Umm . . ." he stated as she performed her new job.

She couldn't stop the tears from rolling down her eyes. *I can't believe I'm doing this,* she thought.

He finally came and she got off of him. Feeling disgraced, she wiped her eyes, put her shorts back on, and quickly exited the vehicle. Even though she'd used the feminine wipes Mimi told her to use, she still never felt dirtier in her life.

Chapter Seventeen

With only thirty seconds remaining in the game, Joe's team was ahead 84-52. Joe knew that they had a pact to keep beef away from the charity game, but he wasn't going to let this opportunity to demean Sweets slip away. He stood up and looked at Sweets. He then put up his middle finger and cracked a small smile.

Sweets was steaming hot. He hated to lose, and to lose to Joe made it that much worse. Sweets stared at Joe as he openly disrespected him in front of the entire audience.

Someone in the crowd stood up and yelled, "North Side!"

Other members of the crowd began to chant, "North Side!" giving respect to Joe's side of the city.

Sweets, totally humiliated, wasn't going to let Joe's disrespect ride. He looked over at the members of the Shottah Boyz, and Rah-Rah nodded his head, to signal that he would take care of the problem.

Malek dribbled the ball, waiting for the final buzzer to sound. He had easily led his team to a victory. When the final buzzer went off, everyone cleared the stands and rushed the court, chanting, "North Side, North Side, North Side."

Malek smiled and scanned the crowd. He went over to Joe and gave him a brief hug, and the team joined him, huddling around and jumping up and down.

Joe embraced Malek and locked hands with him. "Good game, fam. You did ya thing out there. You ever need something or a favor, holla at me."

"Thanks."

The crowd had begun to break up, but in the midst of everything, Malek spotted her. He spotted Halleigh and his heart dropped.

"I'm 'bout to let that bitch-ass nigga have it," Rah-Rah said under his breath. He gripped on his .45 pistol that he had tucked under his shirt. The youngest of the Shottah Boyz, he was by far the nuttiest of the clique. Rah-Rah watched Jamaica Joe as he embraced one of the players from his team and knew that it was the perfect time to get at him. He had the go-ahead from Sweets to let him have it and was more than happy to put in the work. Rah-Rah got within five feet of Joe, pulled out his pistol and pointed it at him, while he was still embracing Malek.

* * *

Halleigh felt dirty as she rushed away from the car, and it seemed as though people were staring at her. It was like they knew what she'd just done.

Mitch emerged from the car and ran after her. He yelled, "Yo, ma!"

She stopped walking and turned around to face him, but didn't respond. She knew that she had hit a new low. In her wildest dreams, she never thought she would turn a trick. What was happening to her? Who was she becoming? She didn't even know herself anymore.

"Where can I reach you, you know, if I'm trying to see you again?" Mitch asked. "I mean, you working for somebody, or is this a private hustle?"

"I work for Manolo." She hated what she had just said. *I work for Manolo.* She never wanted to work for him. She just wanted him to love and protect her from the very mean streets he now had her working. Tears flooded her eyes.

"Word? You a Manolo 'mami'?" he asked. Before she could respond, he continued, "Damn, that nigga is moving up. Let him know Mitch said you good for business, baby. He ain't had a bitch like you since Tash retired." Mitch pulled off another hundred-dollar bill and placed it in her hand. "I'm-a get at you again, ma, for real."

Halleigh placed the money down in her short's pocket with the other bills as she stood on the curb. Just as she was getting ready to go find Mimi, gunshots rang out through the park. *Boom! Boom! Boom!*

157

The park suddenly turned into a frenzy as everybody began ducking low and running for cover. Pandemonium reigned. The thunder of feet stampeding and hysterical shouts could be heard all over the park.

Oh, God! Where is Mimi? She looked frantically for Tasha, Manolo, and Mimi. Anybody. But when she didn't find them, she made a run for the car.

Boom! Boom! More shots rang out.

Mimi spotted Halleigh running toward the car, which she had already made her way to. She yelled, "Hal! Hal! Come on. Them niggas started shooting. Somebody got shot! The police on they way."

Manolo, who was sitting in the driver's side of the car, along with Tasha in the front passenger side, yelled, "Halleigh, let's go!"

Halleigh finally hopped into the car. Tasha was sitting calmly on the passenger's side, and when everyone was safely inside, she called out, "All right, let's go." And Manolo pulled away from the curb and headed toward the house.

After they all calmed down, Tasha turned toward the back seat. She could tell by the look on Halleigh's face that she'd been crying. Her eyes were red. But Tasha knew that those tears had nothing to do with the fear of bullets traveling. *She turned her first trick.* Tasha recognized the lost look that every girl had after they turned their first trick.

As if Manolo had read Tasha's mind, he said pointedly, "Hal, I saw you handling your business out there. You got my money?"

Halleigh pulled the money from her pocket and handed it to Manolo.

He looked at the four crisp hundred-dollar bills. "Damn, Hal! How much you charge the nigga?"

"Two fifty. He just told me to keep the rest," she answered in a whisper. Dazed, she stared blankly out of the window.

Manolo laughed and looked in the rearview at the young girl. Then he looked at Mimi, who sat next to her. "You see that? You better take notes." Manolo was pleased with himself for grooming a bitch like Halleigh. He knew she was guaranteed to make him money.

Looking at her through the rearview mirror as she stared out of the window, he knew that out of all the girls, she really wasn't cut out for this business. For a brief moment, a little bit of guilt seeped into his veins, but then he thought about his mother, eloquently referred to as Lady. Lady—she resembled the legendary Lady Day, Billie Holiday, before heroin took its toll on her looks—was a high-yellow hustler, and Manolo's father was her pimp. So if hoeing was good enough for his mother, it was certainly good enough for any bitch. And with that thought, the guilt evaporated from his veins as he visualized just how much money his little Sunshine was really worth.

Chapter Eighteen

The shots rang out as Malek was embracing Joe. *Boom! Boom!*

"What the fuck was that?" Joe hollered. He let Malek go, but Malek's body acted as if it didn't want to part from Joe's, as if it was just heavy and couldn't move.

Just then, Malek, clinging to Joe, said as loudly as he could, which turned out to be a whisper, "Man, I've been hit!"

His tone was so low, and the whole park had fallen into such chaos, Joe didn't hear him. "Get up off me!" Joe exclaimed, unaware that Malek had been hit. Once again, he tried to push Malek off him.

Bullets that were, in fact, meant for Joe, had caught Malek in the calf and in his hip, but no one noticed, as people emerged from every direction, running and hiding. Screams rang out and echoed throughout the park; the cacophony of gunfire piercing the summer day making it sound like the Fourth of July. Except, these were no firecrackers.

The park had erupted into a war zone. People fell to the ground, and some hid behind cars as they called out to one another to try to get to safety.

"Hit the ground."

"Run!"

"Get Nay-Nay and them."

Instantly, Joe's henchmen came to their boss's defense, and they began to return fire. Laying there in the midst of gunfire, Malek listened to the curses of Joe's men. "Aw, hell naw!" one called out. "No, these bitch-ass niggas didn't start no shit today of all days."

"Open fire on these mu'fuckas," another spat.

"I swear on everything I love, it's on," another one said.

Rah-Rah shouted, "Y'all niggas is dead." He maneuvered through the crowd, smoking gun in his hand. He'd heard shots fired and knew that they were coming for him. He saw his older brother, Lynch, another member of the Shottah Boyz, trading shots with one of Joe's henchmen.

Boom! Boom!

Rah-Rah rose up and fired two shots at Tariq, who was shooting it out with his brother. Rah-Rah bust his gun like a madman, not caring who he hit, as he continued to fire in Tariq's direction carelessly.

Meantime, women, children, and men scattered in a frenzy, trying not to get caught by stray bullets.

"Yo, I'm hit," Malek whispered, holding his leg in agony. It felt like a missile had hit him. He had fallen on top of Joe when he got hit.

After pushing Malek off him, Joe held the young man in his arms. He looked at his leg and noticed that the bullet had gone in and out, and that blood was pouring out of his calf. "It went in and out. You good. Stay right here!"

Joe then reached into his waist and pulled out his all-black .45 pistol. He cocked it and rose up. Without even ducking for cover, he walked straight toward Rah-Rah, who was too busy busting at Tariq to see him coming. With one shot, Joe sent a hollow-tip through Rah-Rah's torso, causing him to drop his gun and fall to the pavement. He then walked over to Rah-Rah as he spat up blood and clenched his stomach.

As Rah-Rah struggled to get air, Joe stared at the young boy. He pointed his gun at Rah-Rah's head, his index finger on the trigger, and his conscience pricked him. *This kid doesn't even look a day older than seventeen*, he thought to himself. Mayhem happening all around him, he blocked all of it out and just stared deep into Rah-Rah's eyes as the young boy tried to stay conscious. Joe looked at the tattoo on the boy's neck—*Shottah Boyz*. He then realized that the young boy wasn't an average kid. He was a killer. A killer who had just tried to take his life. Joe let off two bullets into Rah-Rah's chest, leaving him staring into space forever.

Joe saw the rest of the members of the Shottah Boyz jump into a black tinted SUV and speed off. He ran back toward Malek, who was on the ground in pain. He yelled to his henchmen across the park, "Yo, come over here!"

His workers, along with Tariq, ran over to him and picked up Malek so they could rush him to the hospital. But when the screeching tires of the black SUV that the Shottah Boyz had jumped into came back around, Joe and his men immediately began to fire shots at the truck, but the bullets didn't penetrate.

"It's bulletproof!" Joe yelled. He stopped firing. He knew he'd just be wasting shots. He was very familiar with bulletproof whips, since all of his were equipped with the feature.

The back door opened, and a young man that strongly resembled Rah-Rah came out with his hands up and no shirt on, to let them know he wasn't strapped. Tears ran down his eyes as he slowly walked toward his dead brother.

Joe signaled his crew to take Malek to the car and to not shoot at Lynch. He understood the game.

"No! Oh, my God. Rah-Rah!" Lynch held both hands above his head and made his way over to his younger brother. He wasn't even focused on the men who had been shooting at him with their guns. He just wanted to come and get his heart—his brother. He didn't notice that Rah-Rah wasn't in the car, until they reached the corner and he knew that something had gone wrong. Rah-Rah was the fastest of them all and was always the first to jump in the car when they exited a crime scene. But not this time. He had an inevitable appointment with his maker.

Lynch had come back, unconcerned for any danger to himself, and found his brother lying dead. He kneeled next to his brother's lifeless body and gently scooped him into his arms and rocked back and forth. He hadn't cried since adolescence, but now he was crying a river for Rah-Rah, another soul lost to the game.

Malek heaved deep breaths and squirmed in the back seat as Tariq sped through Flint's streets, headed toward McLaren Hospital. The bullet wound felt like fire.

Joe, sitting next to Malek, tried to keep him calm. "You gon' be all right, fam. Just hold steady."

Malek tried to block out the pain, but it was too much to bear. The only thing he could think about was how his basketball future and life with Halleigh were doomed. His life was going in a fast downward spiral. This was the beginning of the end for him.

Chapter Nineteen

Malek rested in his hospital bed as his mother sat next to him with her Bible open. His father had just left after Mrs. Johnson insisted he go home and get some rest. He agreed, but only upon the promise that, once he returned to the hospital, she would go home and get some rest too. Mrs. Johnson had been right there by Malek's side for days straight. She hadn't even changed clothes, she was so worried about her son.

The room was filled with flowers from Jamaica Joe and his crew.

"Even though I walk through the valley of the shadow of death, I fear no evil," Mrs. Johnson read from Psalm 23:4.

"Ma, stop reading all that stuff about dying. I'm gon' be fine," Malek assured her.

"I know. The doctor said you were lucky. This

has always been one of my favorite scriptures, though. It's comforting."

Mrs. Johnson had been reading him her favorite scriptures for the past three days. She'd almost had a heart attack when she got news that her only son had been shot. She was relieved when the doctor informed her that both wounds had been in-and-out and no major organs had been punctured. Malek was very lucky to not have any permanent damage.

One reason Mrs. Johnson had been continuously reading scripture was because she felt that if she kept talking, Malek wouldn't have time to ask her what she knew he had been wondering about for the past three days. But finally, she had worked up the nerve to tell Malek what she knew was his greatest fear.

"Baby," Mrs. Johnson started, "your, uh, agent called me this morning." She swallowed the knot in her throat.

Malek sat up at attention. "What did he say?" Malek had wondered why his agent hadn't been up to the hospital to see him, and was fearing the worst. That he was no longer interested in agenting him.

"He, uh, said that, uh—"

"Come on, Ma," Malek said, starting to get agitated, "just spit it out."

"Okay, son, he said that all the NBA teams have lost interest in you," Mrs. Johnson reluctantly informed Malek, and it just broke her heart to do so.

She knew that the news would hurt his heart just as well, but she had to tell him the truth.

"What?" Malek said as he sat there in shock. The words felt like daggers straight through his heart.

"Baby, I'm sorry," Mrs. Johnson said. "He said it doesn't look too good. He doesn't even want to represent you anymore."

A single tear slid down Malek's face as his childhood dreams began to evaporate. All he knew was basketball. If you took that away from him, in his mind, he was nothing.

"Let's just thank the Almighty Lord that you are still breathing." Mrs. Johnson grabbed her only child's hand.

Malek was too devastated to speak. He just threw his head back in the pillow, bit his bottom lip, and let the tears flow. He didn't have Halleigh, he didn't have basketball, and he didn't have any hope. College basketball was out of the question, because he'd hired an agent, which made him ineligible to play college ball. And the bullet holes in his body wasn't helping matters, either.

"Ma, the only thing I ever wanted to do was play ball. That's all I ever knew. What am I supposed to do now, huh? I was supposed to buy you and Dad that big brick house. I'm just like my real daddy now. A failure."

"Malek, hush that nonsense. You ain't nothing like that man. You are an intelligent young man with all the opportunities in the world. This little mishap isn't going to stop you. With God on our side, we gon' make it through this, hear?"

"Yes, ma'am." Malek gripped his mother's hand. "Ma, I never forgot how you worked so hard all these years. And how Pops worked those two jobs selling sweepers and doing telemarketing sales just to feed and clothe me. How y'all found the money to send me to basketball camp every summer, even if y'all had to go without. Mama, I will try to find some way to pay you and Dad back, I promise." Malek just broke down in a heaving sob.

"Don't worry about it. Everything is going to work out. You don't owe me or your father anything. Just be a good man and make something out of your life. I don't know why this happened to you, son, but we are going to get through it."

Malek didn't tell his mother that he knew the man who the bullet was really intended for. He just told her that he was at the wrong place at the wrong time and caught a stray bullet, trying to spare her all that worrying.

The painkillers the doctor had Malek on were starting to make him kind of drowsy. As he began to doze off, the thoughts of the news about his future was eating him up.

"I love you, baby," Mrs. Johnson said, rubbing her son's forehead.

"I love you too," Malek answered, closing his eyes.

Malek thoughts were consumed by his ugly reality. Why hadn't he listened to his agent, or to his own gut feelings for that matter? He'd had a bad feeling about playing in the Berston game, but felt that he owed it to Joe. Now his career had ended before it even began.

I fucked up. I fucked up, Malek thought to himself, wishing that the recent events had never happened. But Mrs. Johnson was right. At least he had his life, unlike Rah-Rah, who his brother, Lynch, could only wish for at this point. Three days after the shooting, Malek might have been laying up in the hospital, but Lynch's brother was about to be laying six feet under.

Lynch walked out of the funeral home with revenge on his mind. He just had to do the most difficult task he'd ever been faced with—pick out his brother's casket. He didn't know how he would even make it through the funeral. It had always been Rah-Rah and Lynch, since they were little boys. He didn't know how he was going to be able to go on.

Although grief-stricken, all he could think about for the last three days was getting back at Jamaica Joe. He kept picturing him hugging and cheering along with Malek after the game. The more he thought about it, the angrier he became.

Still feeling incensed, he joined Sweets and the rest of the Shottah Boyz in Sweet's Hummer. He wanted Jamaica Joe's blood. "Where you say ol' dude live again?" Lynch asked. He loaded up his automatic assault rifle, aka, the street sweeper.

Sweets hadn't been able to find out where Joe lived, so he suggested the next best thing. He was going to make Joe look for them. "Yeah, when you wanna bring out a rat, you gotta lay out the cheese," Sweets told Lynch. "Don't worry, we gon' get these niggas. I swear on everything I love, and I swear on your brother's grave."

Sweets was also devastated by the loss. Rah-Rah had been like a son to him. He had raised the boy up since he was nine years old. After their mother's crack habit had caused her to dissipate into a strawberry, Rah-Rah and Lynch were just two homeless little waifs.

Although they had been placed in foster care, the boys kept running away due to the physical and emotional abuse. When Sweets found them, they had just run away from their latest foster home placement and were eating out of the garbage. He took them into his home and taught them a trade. Eventually, the authorities, their caseloads swollen with too many drug babies, too many broken families, and too much dysfunction to worry about two little black boys, stopped looking for them. So they were just another statistic that had fallen into the cracks.

From the start, Sweets became their provider, their protector, and their mentor. Sweets never forgot the foster home he had been raised in, where he had been sexually molested. Which was why he had always provided a safe haven for "his boys." Although bisexual, Sweets wasn't a pedophile, and he never messed with any of his boys. That's why they were all so loyal to him. In return, they became his little killing squad; Rah-Rah being the baddest.

Sweets never went along with his Shottah Boyz

when handling business, but this time it was personal. He was ready to kill anyone associated with Joe, and that meant Malek was in danger now too.

After some convincing from the nurses on staff, Mrs. Johnson went home to get some rest. They told her that the medication would have Malek out for quite some time, so while he was asleep, it was as good a time to sleep as any for her as well. At first, she insisted that she do what she had been doing, sleeping right there in the hospital chair, but after further convincing she headed on home.

Mrs. Johnson pulled up to her house and prepared to walk in to change clothes. She wanted to get back to her son's side as quickly as possible. She knew that he was in pain. She didn't show Malek, but she was hurting inside also. The thought of a big house was nice to her. She didn't say it, but she had also been banking on Malek getting drafted by the pros.

She had worked hard for so many years, and she thought that Malek would change all of that. But reality finally set in, and she now knew the chances of him going pro were slim and next to nothing.

It took all her strength not to break down and cry when she pulled up in front of their little Cape Cod-style house. Malek just didn't know what his success had represented for her. He'd been her entire life, and his success had become hers.

Now, she could see the dark days that lay ahead for her son. She was a realist. It was a crushing defeat for her to see Malek throw away his one opportunity to get out of Flint.

Nineteen years earlier, she had missed her chance when she chose not to go away to college, hooking up instead with Malek's biological father, which turned out to be one of the worst decisions, considering he never was a father to her son. Determined not to raise her child on welfare, she worked at a string of low-paying jobs, never the career she could have had as a school teacher, had she not chosen love. That's why she didn't want Malek to throw everything away on a hoodrat like Halleigh, who was no longer in the picture anyhow.

Mrs. Johnson was so consumed by her thoughts as she shambled up the stairs on her front porch and unlocked her front door, she didn't see the black SUV pull up with Lynch hanging out of the window, his weapon cocked.

Shots rang out as Lynch sprayed the house like an insane man. He didn't care that he was shooting at an innocent bystander. He just wanted to send a message to Joe. Bullets ripped through Mrs. Johnson's back, and she fell to the ground, gripping her Bible to her chest.

"Lord, help me," were her last words spoken.

Lynch made the Johnson house look like Swiss cheese and laughed as he let off his whole clip. He was trying to start a war. And indeed that's what he did. The war had just begun—North versus South Flint.

Chapter Twenty

"You got another john on his way up," Tasha said into the phone.

"Okay, I'm ready." Halleigh watched her last customer leave the room. She hung up the phone and took a long, deep breath. She walked over to the hotel's bathroom so she could freshen up before her next customer arrived. She glanced in the mirror and didn't recognize the face that was staring back at her.

The past weeks had flown by like a blur and she hated the person that she had become. What would her momma think if she saw her little girl now? What would Malek think? she wondered. Or was he even thinking about her at all? But she knew one thing. Not a day went by when Malek didn't cross her mind.

I can't believe he just up and left me like that. He promised me that he would always be here for me. I should've never told him about what happened that night. He probably thought less of me because—

Before Halleigh could complete her thoughts, the sound of knocking on the door filled the air. She dropped her head and rested her hands on the sink as she remembered how much she hated exchanging sex for money. But it was the only way she knew to survive.

Halleigh wiped the semen from her cheek as she finished up her last job for the day. The overweight black man was looking at her with goo-goo eyes as he stroked his manhood until all of his juices were out.

"You something else, Sunshine!" he said, calling her by her working name, the one Manolo had branded her with. He pulled up his pants and zipped them up.

Halleigh looked at Barry and smiled as she stood to her feet. Barry was a regular customer of hers who loved to frequently call upon her to get a blowjob after work. She was totally disgusted by him, but she would never let him know that. Let Barry tell it, Halleigh enjoyed hitting him off just as much as he loved receiving it.

"Eighty dollars, Daddy." Halleigh walked over to the bathroom sink totally nude, her voluptuous cakes shifting sides with every step.

Barry enjoyed the view and left a hundred-dollar bill on the bed, giving her a twenty-dollar tip. "See you next week, baby," he said, admiring Halleigh's body. He headed for the door to return to his wife and children across town.

"I'll be waiting for you, Daddy," she said, leaning halfway out of the bathroom and displaying her pretty smile. She glanced at the bed to make sure he had left her the cash and then focused back on him as he exited the hotel room.

As soon as the door closed behind him, she dropped her fake smile and went over to pick up her cash. She was glad that it was the end of the day so she could rest. She'd turned eight tricks that day, and her body was tired. After turning her first trick with Mitch, she had started keeping count, but now there had been so many, she'd lost count of how many tricks she'd turned in the past weeks.

She turned on the shower and flopped on the bed. She picked up the phone and called Tasha to let her know she had finished up with her last client. Tasha instructed her to meet her in her room when she finished showering.

After getting fresh, Halleigh walked to Tasha's room and knocked on the door.

"Come in. It's open!" she heard Tasha yell.

Halleigh opened the door and saw Tasha on the bed counting money. She had money stacks placed all over the bed as she sat Indian-style adding up the day's total. Halleigh couldn't understand why Tasha didn't have to turn tricks anymore, but although Tasha was only twenty-three, she had put in a lot of work for Manolo. She had been turning tricks since she was sixteen, and Manolo had a sweet spot for her.

"Hey, girl," Tasha said as she looked at Halleigh with a smile. "How did you do tonight?"

"Not too bad. I made nearly eight hundred," Halleigh replied, digging into her purse and pulling out a wad of money.

Tasha, still counting the money, replied, "Toss it on the bed."

Following Tasha's instructions, Halleigh stated, "Girl, I'm tired as hell. I hate when you send stanky-ass Barry to me."

"That nigga is fat and ugly as hell, but the nigga always request you. That's a part of the game though." Tasha briefly stopped counting the money and looked at Halleigh. "Nolo gon' be happy with you. You made a killing tonight."

"Yeah, they were tipping good."

Mimi came storming in, a Newport hanging out of her mouth. "What's up, bitches?" Mimi said jokingly. She kicked off her stilettos. "These mu'-fuckas are killing my feet."

"Hey, Mimi," Halleigh said as she watched Mimi dig into her bra and pull out wrinkled bills.

"Hey, girl," Tasha said while she counted the money.

"I made five hundred tonight," Mimi said, tossing money onto the bed near Tasha. "Damn, I'm good!" She looked at Halleigh. "How much you make?"

Tasha replied on Halleigh's behalf, "Eight hundred."

Mimi got a salty look on her face and smacked her lips in jealousy. Tasha and Halleigh giggled at the sight of Mimi's bubble getting busted.

"Anyways!" Mimi said as she snapped her head

and rolled her eyes, and she and Tasha began a conversation while Halleigh's mind was elsewhere.

Halleigh couldn't believe the life she was leading. She could've been preparing to graduate from school and be with the love of her life. But instead she was laid up in a cheap hotel, fucking anybody who was willing to throw her a little cash. *I can't believe I was stupid enough to fall for Manolo's game. He took advantage of my situation, and now I can't get out. I wish I would have run away from his ass the day I met him,* she thought sadly to herself. Halleigh, ashamed of the things she was doing, knew that she had to get by any way that she could.

"Y'all coming to watch my set tonight?" Mimi asked. She often doubled up and made money in Manolo's and Sweets' strip club. She was all about her paper and figured that if she was gon' sell pussy, she might as well get extra customers from Wild Thangs.

Halleigh was so engrossed in her own thoughts that she didn't even hear Mimi. The only thing on her mind at that particular moment was Malek. She missed him, and the thought of him hurt so badly, she tried to suppress the fact that she ever had him in her life. *Ain't no point in thinking about what I can't have,* she thought.

"Damn, Hal, what you thinking about?" Tasha asked. "You good, girl?"

"Yeah, I'm good," she replied.

Mimi just stared at her. That wasn't the first time she'd seen Halleigh just completely blank out. She knew what the cause was too. Halleigh was heartbroken. "Fuck that nigga, Hal," Mimi remarked. "He didn't deserve you anyway. I bet you his ass ain't losing no sleep over you."

Tasha looked at Halleigh. "What nigga?"

Halleigh lowered her eyes to the floor and shook her head. "Nobody," she said.

"It better be nobody. I hope you not talking about the kid, Malek. Manolo will kill both you and him if he even finds out you even thinking about him."

"But he's not gon' find out," Mimi cut in quickly. "Right, Tash?"

Tasha looked at Halleigh. "Yeah, I'll keep my mouth shut, but you get your head together, Hal."

Halleigh tried to dismiss thoughts of Malek. "Ain't nothing to get together, Tasha. Don't worry, I'm okay."

Tasha almost felt bad for Halleigh as she watched her drift back into wishful thinking. She knew that Halleigh wasn't built for the lifestyle she was leading. *It takes a strong bitch to make this money. You can't let it make you,* Tasha thought. She knew that Halleigh looked down on herself for what she had become, and it was the first time that she felt guilty for keeping one of Manolo's girls in line.

"Let's get out of here." Tasha stood and walked out of the room, heading toward home.

When they arrived at the house, Tasha went to give Manolo their earnings for the night. She tapped on his door lightly and then entered without waiting for a response. When she opened the door she saw Manolo kicked back on his king-size bed, one hand down his sweat pants, the other on the remote control.

"Bring that ass over here," he ordered.

Tasha chortled and then walked over to the bed. She could tell that he had blown a couple trees from the scent of marijuana that still lingered in the air.

"You already know what I want," he said, patting a spot on the bed next to him.

"Yeah, I know." She pulled out and then dumped the rolled-up wads of money onto the bed beside him.

Manolo grabbed the cash and began counting, *twenty, forty, sixty, sixty-five, seventy* . . . until he reached two thousand seven hundred.

"How much Mimi bring in?" he asked, a look of confusion on his face.

Tasha noticed. "Five—why you ask that?"

He ignored her question, but in his head he thought, *That bitch been shaving money off the top. She usually brings in at least seven bills a night.*

Once Tasha saw that he wasn't going to respond to her, she got up to leave.

Before she reached the door, he said, "Send Halleigh in here. I feel like getting my dick sucked."

Tasha turned up her face. She hated when Manolo got beside himself. He usually treated his girls decent, but when something was bothering him, he would get to smelling hisself and start degrading his girls. She nodded and then walked out of the room.

Tasha entered the room Halleigh and Mimi

shared in time to see Mimi standing with her back to the mirror and her head turned around as she watched herself work her ass muscles. She wore only a thong and was making her booty clap.

"Them other hoes don't got shit on me. Them bitches better hope my set ain't first, cuz it ain't gon' be no tip money left," Mimi mumbled conceitedly.

Mimi was a different type of chick. She was confident and felt like she chose to do what she was doing. Her motto was, "If I'm a ho, I'm a top-dollar ho," and she didn't mind sleeping with a different man every night as long as his pockets were heavy.

Tasha wished that Manolo had asked her to get Mimi for him instead of Halleigh, since she was beside herself as well. She knew that Halleigh wasn't built for hoeing and sooner or later it would break her. And she didn't need Manolo throwing her no extra work. "Hal, Nolo wants you," Tasha stated.

Halleigh nodded and then left the room. She walked into Manolo's room and she could see the print of his hard dick through his baggy sweat pants. "Tasha said you wanted me." Her tone was dead as she walked over and sat on the bed next to him.

He pulled out his manhood and began to stroke himself. "Hook me up, baby girl."

The thought of pleasing Manolo almost made her gag. Now that she realized how he had played her, she was disgusted by him. She hated to be in the same room with him because he reminded her of all the things that had gone wrong in her life since losing Malek. Now whenever she looked at

Manolo he reminded her of the rape because he left her feeling just as powerless. At least when she was raped, she fought back until the two men overpowered her. Now, it was like she was getting screwed in the ass, straight up, with no Vaseline. And it was like she had given him permission. As bad as her mother's drug habit was, as far as Halleigh knew, Sharina had never turned tricks for a living. She mainly got her money through boosting.

"Nolo, I have to get ready to go to the club," she said in avoidance.

"I own the mu'fucka. That can wait." He grabbed the back of her neck and slowly pulled her head into his lap. When she pulled in the opposite direction, he applied more force. "What are you running from, Halleigh? I said put your mouth on it!" he whispered through clenched teeth. As the words came out, he gripped her hair and pulled roughly.

"Oww! Manolo, you hurting me!" she yelled as she resisted more.

A few minutes later, Tasha and Mimi heard an ear-piercing scream that came out of Manolo's room. "Agghhh!!!"

"What is he doing to her?" Mimi asked.

Tasha hurried into Manolo's room. Halleigh was laid over the bed fighting against Manolo as he grabbed for her panties.

"Daddy, Daddy, wait!" Tasha reached for Manolo's raised fist as he prepared to strike Halleigh.

He pushed Tasha off of him and continued his rage against Halleigh. "You telling me no? How you gon' tell me I can't have what's mine?" he yelled.

He bitch-slapped Halleigh in the mouth before she knew what had happened.

Just as he was about to hit Halleigh again, Tasha flung herself over her, blocking Manolo's blow. "Wait, Daddy, she didn't mean it. Halleigh hasn't been feeling too good. She's just tired. She made you eight hundred dollars today all by herself. She just don't want you to be in no stanky pussy, Daddy. She just wanna be fresh for you. She worked hard for you today." Tasha was rambling and talking so fast, Manolo actually bought the bullshit that she was selling.

Halleigh was sniffling and crying violently.

"Go help her fix her shit up. We got to be at the club in thirty minutes!" he yelled.

Tasha quickly pulled Halleigh out of the room.

Manolo slammed the door behind them, but not before they heard him mumble, "Ungrateful-ass bitch!"

"Are you all right?" Mimi asked Halleigh when they came back into her room.

Halleigh couldn't stop crying. She hated her life. *How did I get here?* she asked herself.

"She's fine. Help me clean her up," Tasha said.

Halleigh had a busted lip, and Mimi quickly went to retrieve a washcloth to wipe up the blood. She also grabbed Tasha's makeup kit.

"What were you thinking," Tasha asked her, "boss'n up on Manolo? When he asks for something, you give it to him—plain and simple."

"I can't," Halleigh choked out words in between her tears.

184

"What you mean, you can't? You better." Mimi began to put makeup on Halleigh. "And quit crying. You fucking up my work."

Halleigh held the tears inside. "I can't do this no more. This is not me. This is not how my life was supposed to be."

Tasha turned Halleigh's head toward her so she could look her in the eyes. "Listen, Hal, you have to get yourself together. This may not be what you had planned, but this is what you got. You better deal with whatever you going through before you get yourself hurt. Manolo don't play that shit. You the one told him that he could do this to you. Now you got to live with your decision."

"I told him? I didn't tell him he could pimp me," Halleigh said in a harsh whisper. Visions of how she could have been at prom with Malek, or how she could now be walking across the stage at her graduation to get her diploma danced through her mind.

"You told him that he was Daddy. You gave him permission to do this to you. You have to just accept it and get used to it. There is no way out, Hal. He will kill you before he lets you leave. All you have to do is do what he tells you, and you will be fine, I promise," Tasha stated. "Okay?"

Halleigh nodded, and both girls embraced her to make her feel better.

"Okay, okay! Let's go, so y'all bitches can watch me work," Mimi stated with a smile, trying to lighten the mood.

Chapter Twenty-one

When Manolo and the girls had first entered the club, 50 Cent's "Hustler's Ambition" was blasting. The crowd swayed back and forth to the rhythm.

Meanwhile, people addressed Mimi as though she were a hood celebrity. One patron called out, "Mimi, you on tonight?"

Mimi nodded and then went straight to the dressing room to prepare for her set. Manolo, Tasha, and Halleigh sat in the large booth of the strip joint as they all waited for Mimi to come on stage.

The club was crowded, and everyone seemed to be having a good time. The club's patrons consisted of many of the major Flint players, hustlers, pimps and whores. The women wore mini dresses, jumpsuits, and capri pants, and the men wore anything from suits to casual wear. All the pimps wore bright colors, from canary yellow to parakeet green, carried gold canes, and wore different styles of hats to distinguish themselves.

"You okay, Hal?" Tasha asked as she leaned in toward her to whisper the words in her ear.

Halleigh nodded, but Tasha knew differently. She could tell that Halleigh was uncomfortable. Her body language said it all. She sat with her hands tucked tightly in between her legs and she hadn't said a word all night. Tasha hoped that the young girl would develop a thick skin. Otherwise, she'd never make it. *She has to if she wants to survive in this game.* Tasha stared at Halleigh with a sympathetic look in her eyes. *As much money as she is pulling in, Manolo ain't trying to cut her loose no time soon.*

Tasha was familiar with Manolo's tactics. First, he lured the young girls in. He made them feel as if he would take care of them even though no one else wanted them. Although his girls knew that he was a pimp, he always made each one feel as if she was more special than the next. After he was sure that he was inside their head, he would flip the script on them. He would remind them of all the things that he'd done for them and make them feel indebted to him. It was never too long before he put a girl to work. He also knew how to keep them pitted against each other with suspicion and envy. By the time these girls realized they were being pimped, it was too late. Manolo had them so afraid of him that they did it just to avoid upsetting him.

Tasha knew the game well because she had been through it. She was different than the other girls, though. She was strong-minded and let Manolo know up front that she wasn't trying to trick her entire life.

They came up with the agreement that if she watched over the other girls and helped him keep them in line, then he wouldn't put her to work. Tasha was twenty-three and hadn't turned a trick in almost three years. In fact, she was instrumental in Manolo's operation, helping to instill the fear in the rest of his girls. With Halleigh it was different, though. She now felt guilty for trapping the young girl.

A half-hour had gone by before Mimi finally came on stage. That's when the DJ, on cue, began to spin T-Pain's "I'm N Love (Wit A Stripper)." She was wearing a "Catwoman" outfit and glasses before she slowly stripped down to her thong. All eyes were on her as she hopped to the top of the pole, intertwining her legs through it and spinning seductively to the bottom. She worked the pole like the professional that she was, seducing the pole like she was handling a hard dick. She also knew how to clap her ass cheeks without missing a beat.

Tasha smirked as she looked around the club and noticed how the men practically worshiped Mimi. She had to admit, *That bitch is good.*

Mimi rolled her stomach as she held onto the pole with one hand. She walked around picking up as many dollar bills as she could without interrupting her entrancing dance. She then turned toward the crowd and did the move she'd practiced at home. Men crowded the stage when her thick ass and thighs jiggled as she made her ass clap.

Mimi wrapped one leg around the neck of one of the spectators and grinded her pussy in his face. It didn't surprise Tasha when the man stuck his tongue out and took a taste of Mimi's spot. She continued to dance in front of him as she held out her hand, waiting for him to bless her with some cash. By the end of the song, she'd made about three hundred easily.

Mimi sashayed off stage and went over to Manolo's table. "How I do, Daddy?" she asked.

"I don't know. You tell me?" he responded, referring to how much money she'd just made.

Mimi discreetly rolled her eyes and pulled out the crumbled bills. Manolo took his cut and then handed the rest back to her. The split was always the same, 80/20 in Manolo's favor.

This nigga always taking all the money, but he don't put in no work, Mimi complained silently.

They all knew that the way the money was cut up was unfair, but no one was stupid enough to say anything to Manolo about it. They signed on to be his mami, and unfortunately, what he said was law.

Manolo sat back, and with Mimi on one side and Halleigh on the other, wrapped his arms tightly around their shoulders. Tasha sat next to Halleigh.

A bright-skinned girl with shoulder-length, kinky hair came walking by. She stopped at the table. "Hey, Daddy, what you drinking?" she asked Manolo.

Tasha rolled her eyes and Mimi gave the girl a dirty look. The girl's name was Keesha. She'd been trying to get down for the longest. She wanted to be a Manolo mami so bad, whenever one of Manolo's girls did something wrong, she was the first to report it to him, hoping he'd get rid of them and allow her to take their place. Her little trick hadn't benefited her thus far, though.

Big nose-ass, snitchin'-ass, stanky-pussy bitch. Mimi crossed her legs. *She want to get down. That bitch is a dirty trick, and her pussy stank, that's why she only serving drinks. Ain't nobody trying to fuck her.*

"Yeah, bring us all some Long Islands, top-shelf, and keep 'em coming. I feel like getting loose tonight," Manolo said.

They all kicked back.

They were having a good time, and even Halleigh began to chill. When she got that liquor in her, she let her guard down and actually forgot about her current circumstances. For a moment, she felt like she was on top of the world. The way Keesha kept pushing up on Manolo, it made her feel like she was a member of an exclusive club. The whole world was the fools and Manolo's mamis were the ones who really had it going on. *Maybe life wasn't so bad after all,* she thought, when the liquor oozed into her bloodstream.

"Uh-oh, here comes this bitch again," Mimi mumbled. She moved over and sat between Tasha and Halleigh.

"Why y'all don't like her?" Halleigh whispered as she watched Keesha approach.

"Uh-um, ain't no *y'all.* Bitch, you don't like her

either," Mimi stated. "That bitch is a snitch and a wannabe." Mimi's lips curled into a sneer of hatred.

Manolo ignored their conversation, but he tightened up when he saw a male approach Mimi. He knew exactly who the baldhead dude was. "What can I do for you, Troy?" he asked, obviously irritated.

"You can't do shit for me," Troy told him. "My business is with li'l mama."

Halleigh looked at Tasha, who looked at Manolo. They all waited for a response.

"She is my business, player. So what can I do for you today, my man?" Manolo took a sip of his drink.

Suddenly, a level of unrest overtook the room. Tension was high at the table, and the girls kept looking back and forth, waiting to see how the situation would play out.

Troy pulled out a badge and flipped it open, along with a hundred-dollar bill. "Look, man, I come in peace. I'm just looking for"—he paused to kiss Mimi's shoulder—"a little entertainment, that's all."

Manolo nodded his head and thought about what he could gain out of having a cop in his pocket. *This dumb mu'fucka will risk his entire career for some pussy. I'm-a make sure I tape this shit.* "I think we can waive the payment under these circumstances." Manolo said. "I'm a man who likes to form business relationships, you know? A favor for a favor. You can have all the entertainment you'd like if you are willing to overlook certain things."

"Consider it done," Troy responded.

Mimi looked on in astonishment. *I know this nigga ain't serious,* she thought to herself. *He 'bout to make me give this pussy up for free?*

Manolo nodded his head as a signal for Mimi to leave with Troy.

She smacked her lips loudly and said, "Fuck that. I ain't messing with no cop. Especially if the mu'fucka ain't paying. Y'all got me fucked up. I'm about to get back to work." She rose from the booth.

Halleigh could see Manolo's temperature rise at Mimi's disrespect.

"Bitch!" he yelled. "You gon' do whatever the fuck I tell you to." He grabbed Mimi's arm forcefully and bent it backwards, as if he was trying to break it.

"Awww!" Mimi cried out.

Tasha immediately jumped up and pulled Mimi into her side of the booth. She stepped over to Troy and whispered in his ear, causing a smile to spread across his face.

"I'll take her," Troy stated, looking Tasha up and down as if he could taste between her legs already.

"I'll take care of him, Daddy," she said to Manolo, getting Mimi off the hook. "Calm down and enjoy your night."

Tasha held on to Troy, who was now palming her ass, and mean-mugged Mimi as she walked away with him. She hadn't had to turn a trick in years and now here she was saving Mimi's ass—literally. *What's happening to me?* Tasha thought. *Since when do I have feeling for these bitches and care whether or not they get their ass kicked by Manolo?*

Tasha could tell by the way Manolo was gritting his teeth that he was furious at Mimi though, and that an ass-kickin' might still be in store for her. Tasha's thoughts continued as she walked away to handle her business with Troy. *This dumb bitch, she don't even know what she just got herself into. Why would she do that shit after what happened earlier with Halleigh telling the nigga no? Now she got me out here about to hit this nigga off just to keep shit peaceful. I ain't tryin'-a fuck with this blue-vested mu'fucka either, but it's all a part of the game.*

Once they were back in the so-called VIP (Very Important Pussy) room, Tasha thought as she lifted her dress and guided Troy's face to her vagina, *Me doing this is gon' keep Mimi's dumb ass out of jail next time. This nigga ain't about to get shit from me. He gon' eat my pussy and beat his own dick. My shit so good, he won't know the difference. If Mimi was as bad as she thinks she is, she wouldn't have to fuck the nigga. Real bitches do real things. You can't be a street diva if you don't know how to make the game work for you.* And that's just what Tasha did, make the game work for her.

194

Chapter Twenty-two

The tension was so thick for the remainder of the night that Halleigh was thankful when it was over.

Manolo had retired to his upstairs office at the club with Tasha, who was more than likely watching him count up the evening's profits, if not counting it herself while he watched over her.

Halleigh and Mimi walked around silently as they helped Keesha clean up. Halleigh was exhausted. It was three in the morning and the club had been dead for about an hour. She couldn't wait to get home, take a shower, and go to bed.

They all looked up when they heard Manolo's footsteps echo through the quiet room. He walked slowly down the steps and approached Mimi, and without saying one word, smacked her clear across the room; his hand making a loud clapping sound when it made contact with Mimi's skin.

"Nolo!" Mimi yelled. "Stop! Don't, Daddy!" She put her hands up to block her face.

Halleigh looked on and witnessed Manolo become a madman, all the nicey-nice façade disappearing, and the real Manolo emerging, as his raging fit took over.

"Bitch, don't you ever," he yelled as his open hand became a fist and he rained punches all over Mimi's body, "in your life . . . disrespect me!"

Halleigh stood frozen in fear; her feet glued to the floor and her mouth as dry as cotton.

Meanwhile, Keesha smirked as Manolo beat Mimi mercilessly, connecting with blow after blow to her body. He hit her repeatedly and made it worse when he grabbed her by her braids so she couldn't block her face. "Bitch, you . . . do . . . what . . . I say do!" he said almost in a patterned rhythm, pausing every time he swung. He was so enraged, he was foaming at the mouth. When his fists became too sore, he stood up and kicked and stomped her.

"Aghh!" she howled from the pain that pierced her small body.

"Manolo!" Tasha yelled, descending the steps two at a time. She'd heard the commotion all the way from upstairs, but she wasn't prepared for the bloody mess that she found downstairs.

Troy ran out behind her, but when he saw Manolo's act, he dismissed himself and left the club. He didn't want to get involved if the police were called in. As an officer, he knew he would be called in to question if he was caught in the red-light district.

"Fuck, Manolo!" Tasha stated as she pulled him off of Mimi. "What did you do to her? How she gon' make you any money now lookin' like this?"

Halleigh was frozen in fear. She watched as Manolo pulled Mimi up by her neck and held her out for everyone to see. "This is what happens to you if you disrespect me." He let Mimi's body drop to the floor.

Tasha rushed to his side. "It's okay, Daddy. Calm down. You taught her. She won't do it again." Tasha pulled Manolo away and led him back up the stairs.

Dumbfounded, Halleigh stared in disbelief at Mimi, who was squirming and moaning in pain on the floor. She was barely conscious.

Tasha snapped her fingers in Halleigh's direction to get her attention. Halleigh finally snapped out of it and looked at Tasha with nothing but pure fear in her eyes. Tasha threw her car keys at Halleigh. "Take her to the house and make sure she's okay." She then turned her attention to Keesha. "And, Keesha, clean this mess up."

Halleigh ran to Mimi's side. "Oh, my God! Mimi!" she whispered. "You'll be okay, Mimi. Come on, let's get you out of here."

"Fuck him," Mimi cried uncontrollably as she spit blood from her mouth.

"Shhh." Halleigh picked Mimi up and put her head underneath her shoulder to support her weight. "We've got to get you out of here."

Mimi limped and could barely walk as they headed

to the car, and when they finally made it, she passed out in the back seat from the pain of her beatdown. Halleigh got in the car and looked in her rearview at Mimi's beaten body. Tears rushed to her eyes. *He could've killed her,* she thought to herself. "It'll be all right. Everything is gon' be okay," she kept repeating; not only trying to convince Mimi, but herself as well. It was times like this that Halleigh wished she'd had a father. If she had one, there was no way she would have been so gullible, getting caught up with the likes of Manolo.

That night in their bedroom, she whispered back and forth with Mimi. "How did you get caught up with Manolo?" she asked her.

"I was just like you, young and dumb. I was trying to get to Hollywood. I wanted to be a dancer. First, he got me in his club, then the next thing I know, he had me on the stroll."

"Do you think we can get away?"

"Only if we leave feet first."

"What's that?"

"Six feet under."

THE END
. . . but the saga continues in
Flint Book 2: Working Girls.

Excerpt

Flint

Book 2:

Working Girls

Chapter One

"Take it or leave it, mu'fucka. It is what it is," Malek stated as he held one hand in his pants and looked up the block to ensure the coast was clear as he interacted with the feind. "You can take yo' ass on the South Side and cop some of that bullshit, or be satisfied with what I just gave your ass," he finished as he waited for his customer to respond, although he knew that eventually, the man would see things his way because Jamaica Joe had the best connect in the city.

The dope fiend examined the bag of heroin, held it up high, and thumbed it, trying to make all of the contents fall to the bottom. The fiend had been complaining about the pack's size, but he knew that he had the best dope in town in the palm of his hands and wasn't going to pass that good high up.

He walked off after leaving Malek with his fifty

dollar, of course, and taking the bag of dope with him. Malek sat on the stoop as he waited for his next customer; not thinking about for one moment, how went from becoming a potential NBA star athlete, to a fuckin' corner boy.

Standing six feet tall, five inches tall, Malek was built for the NBA, but after his mother and stepfather were killed in a drive-by shooting, his distant dream of a budding basketball career died with them. They had been his strength, his rock, his reason for wanting it so bad. They had sacrificed their entire lives for him, and Malek had wanted nothing more than to return their efforts by seeing to it that through his skills and talents, they never had to work again a day in their lives.

Malek was in the hospital recovering from two non-life threatening bullet wounds he had suffered at the Berston Park Battle annual basketball game when he learned of his parent's fate. Bullets from a drive-by shooting riddled his house, killing his mother who was walking up the porch, heading home after spending days in the hospital by Malek's side and his stepfather who had laid asleep on the front living room couch.

With a broken spirit and broken dreams, it wasn't long before Malek fell into the street life full force. Jamaica Joe took him under his wing and put him on the block in seek of the American dream; one that it was obvious his basketball talents wasn't going to get him.

Although Malek's bullet wounds might not have been life threatening, one just happened to bury itself in his leg. He had barely been checked into the hospital before NBA teams, and even colleges, lost interest in him. Even his agent abandoned him in the hospital bed. They feared the inevitable, that his leg would never allow him to play ball like he once had before the ill-fated shooting. Malek now walked with a very slight limp, which camouflaged itself as just part of a smooth swagger.

Malek took to the streets, like a duck took to water and it turned out that he was a natural born hustler. He had only been hustling for a year, but quickly moved up in the ranks. Joe had given him his own block in the Fifth Ward, which was the most profitable block on the North Side of Flint.

Malek rubbed his tattooed neck that had his deceased mother's name written on it, and scanned the block. Everyday Malek thought about his mother and step-father and missed them dearly. The police never found out who was responsible for the fatal shootings, and that hurt Malek even more. Revenge and hatred toward the unknown perpetrator was buried in his bones.

The shooter had taken away every person he had ever loved, with the exception of one; who just seemed to walk away on her own free will, leaving Malek for dead it seemed.

Halleigh was the about the only girl Malek had ever loved. As a matter of fact, it was the night he decided to keep his promise to Halleigh and stand by her side and be there for her that his entire life changed for the worse. And yet she hadn't so much as thought twice about him since.

A silver Lexus pulled onto the block and Malek smiled and threw his hands up, knowing that it was Joe. Joe sat in the passenger seat while his head henchman, Tariq, chauffeured him.

"What's good, son?" Joe asked as he rolled down the window and looked at Malek.

Malek walked over to the car and extended his hand to show Joe love. "What up, fam?" Malek replied, greeting Joe.

"Get in," Joe ordered as he threw his head in the direction of the back seat.

When Malek got in, Tariq gave him an envious stare through the rearview mirror. Tariq didn't care for Malek too much. He was kind of upset at how his boss had taken to the youngster, resulting in Malek getting his own block so quickly. Tariq had to be a corner boy for years before Joe gave him his own block. So he had envy in his heart towards Malek due to the fact that he was given his own block after only a few months. And for Malek to have the busiest block only added to Tariq's jealousy.

"How you do this week?" Joe asked Malek as he lit his blunt while they sat in the idle car talking business.

"I need to re-up again," Malek said as he waved over one of his workers named Trap.

A heavy set hustler about the same age as Malek scanned the block and then reached under the porch and grabbed a brown paper bag. Trap then ran over to the car and handed it to Malek. Malek grabbed the bag and in turn handed it to Joe. Joe opened the bag and money rolls filled it up to the top. He closed the bag and smiled while shaking his head.

"You never cease to amaze me, Malek," Joe said to Malek just as proudly as his stepfather would have congratulated him on winning the NBA championship. "If you keep this up, you're going to be great in this game," Joe said, referring to the dope game.

Joe had never seen anyone move dope like Malek, and he knew that without a doubt Malek was born to hustle. Once again, Joe's intuition that he could benefit greatly from Malek's services paid off. The first time was at Berston Park, where Joe convinced Malek to play on his North Side team in the basketball game battle of which he had fifty grand at stake.

Against Malek's agent's wishes, Malek agreed; not because he wanted to, but because he felt obligated to. After all, Joe was the one who had hired that infamous Flint street attorney that got Malek out of jail for the robbery; a robbery he would have never even thought to attempt in his wildest dreams had it not been for Halleigh.

Thanks to Malek's basketball skills, Joe's team won the game indeed, but that only pissed off his life-long enemy, Sweets, who ran the South Side team; losing his fifty G's to Joe, plus bragging rights he had victoriously retained for the past four games, not to mention his pride. In retaliation, an all out North Side, South Side war broke out after the game. Malek, once again, coming to the rescue of Joe, had taken two bullets that were meant for him instead.

Malek remained silent and glanced at Tariq mugging him through the window.

What's that nigga's problem? Malek thought as he and Tariq exchanged mean stares for a brief moment. *He might just be the problem. I'm going to have to keep an eye on that nigga, Tariq.*

Joe interrupted Malek's thoughts with his next comment. "You ran through a whole brick in two days?" Joe asked Malek, not believing the obvious.

"Yeah. That shit is like clockwork 'round here. I be hitting niggas off proper. I don't be cutting my shit heavy. I might not make as much on the flip, but I run through the dope faster, re-upping more. So in the long run, I make more money," Malek explained strategically.

"If more mu'fuckas thought like you, then everybody could eat off this game." Joe looked to his head henchman. "Ain't that right, Tariq? Not even your ass ever came up with that type of logic." He turned his attention back to Malek, leaving Tariq's ego wounded. "Niggas get greedy and try to stretch they dope so much that it doesn't even get their customers high anymore. I'll have someone drop off a brick in an hour," Joe said as he inhaled the smoke into his lungs.

"No doubt," Malek said, immediately turning the conversation to some more important business. "Have you found out anything about the shooting?" Malek said, questioning Joe for the millionth time about the random drive-by shooting that took his mother's and stepfather's life a year earlier. He was worse than Cealy in *The Color Purple* asking Mista had any mail come for her everyday.

"No, not yet. But trust me, I am going to handle that for you. We're going to make whoever did that pay," Joe answered as Malek then exited the car. "You feel me? You trust me on this one?"

Malek stood outside of the car and looked up to the heavens, where he knew that as much as his mother loved and served the Lord, she was watching down on him. He then looked back down at Joe. "Yeah, I trust you, man."

"That's what I'm talking about." Joe stuck out his hand to give Malek some dap, and then signaled for Tariq to drive off.

Joe and Malek had grown a close bond since the death of Malek's parents. After he lost all potential to go pro, Malek fell into the arms of the streets. With Joe there grooming him, Malek had risen up in the dope game swiftly, and began to make a name for himself in the drug game instead of the basketball game. He had once been popular at his high school, that he never even graduated from after all that stuff went down with the robbery, jail and the shootings. Instead, he just made money hustling, dedicating his life to the streets. And now turned out by the streets, for Malek, there was no turning back.

Chapter Two

Halleigh waited for her next John in the hotel room. On that particular day, business was slow. Tasha usually sent Johns in the room one after another. Halleigh wasn't complaining though; she needed the break. Her body was tired from the constant sexing of men over the last year.

Halleigh sat in front of the vanity mirror and tears began to flow as she looked into her soulless pupils. She hated the woman that she had become. Once a plain Jane high school honors student with a positive future, with a shoe-in future NBA star, was now selling her body and her soul to any man with the right amount of cash.

Her mascara ran down her cheek as she reached into her blouse and pulled out a small baggy. She emptied the contents on the stand and made it into a straight line with her pinky. Halleigh looked down at the white substance that had just become her acquaintance over the last six months. She started snorting as an escape from the reality she was living, hoping that like Calgon, the feeling would take her away. That it wouldn't be her lying there while every Tom, Dick and Kwalie got on top of her and did their business.

Halleigh couldn't believe she was heading down the same path of drug abuse as her feind-out mother, Sharina, who she hadn't seen since she traded Halleigh's virginity to two thugs for a hit.

The brutal assault had left Halleigh devastated. Her own mother had turned on her. So with nowhere else to turn, she went to where she thought she would be safe and protected; she went to Malek. Her high school sweetheart had promised to take care of her; that he wouldn't let anything happened to her while promising to get her up out of the hood. But look at her now.

"I hate my life. It wasn't supposed to be like this," she whispered as she lowered her head and sniffed the cocaine into her nostrils. She immediately jerked her head back to prevent her nose from running. She had picked up this bad habit from a frequent John she serviced that convinced her it was an escape; the much needed escape her mind had been desiring.

After her initial introduction to the vice, she had developed a steady habit for the drug. Anytime she was feeling down or needed a boost to cope with her profession, she leaned on her "new friend"—cocaine.

The phone rang, startling Halleigh as she was trying to enjoy her high. Halleigh wiped her runny nose and walked over to the phone.

"Hello?" Halleigh answered.

"You got another John coming up. He wants a number two," Tasha said, referring to vaginal sex. They called oral sex number ones and vaginal sex number twos. Twelve's was the total package, meaning the client paid double for anything they wanted sexually.

Halleigh took a deep breath and shook her head from side to side. She was sore and wore out and needed a while to recoup.

"Tash, I just came on my period. I can't do it," Halleigh lied, trying to avoid having to take the job. Tasha knew every girl's cycle like clockwork and knew that Halleigh's period wasn't due for a week or so.

"What you talking about, Hal? You know and I know that you ain't on yet," Tasha replied in a confident tone. "Don't even try that bullshit. This is about making that dough. Now, do you want that tricks dick up in your pussy or Daddy's foot up in your ass?"

Halleigh knew that Tasha was right. Manolo, just like most pimps, was known for his short temper with the girls when it came to fucking up his money or just simply not following the rules and being obedient. Halleigh thought about that time when she had first started in the business and Manolo had beaten her down after she refused to please him orally. Then, just like now, she had been worn out and tired after spending an entire day with Johns.

But even as she reflected back on the beating, as tired as she was, she thought the beat down just might be worth it.

"My body has been acting funny lately. I haven't been getting a lot of rest, Tash, you know that," Halleigh replied to a whiny voice, hoping to gain her madame's sympathy.

Tasha felt bad for Halleigh and knew that she needed a break, but she also knew that Manolo would have a problem with that. If it wasn't for Tasha coming to the rescue that time Manolo beat Halleigh, the nineteen-year-old might not even be alive today. Tasha couldn't help but fear what would happen if Manolo got a hold of her again, and this time she wasn't there to protect her.

"Look, you can take the rest of the day off and get yourself together," Tasha told Halleigh before adding a stipulation. "But you have to stay in the room so that Manolo won't find out. I'll send your clients to some of the other girls."

"Thank you so much, Tash. I owe you." Halleigh was glad that she had found favor in Tasha's sight. When Halleigh first started working for Manolo, she saw Tasha as some hardcore, feeling-less broad who cared about two things only: Manolo and Manolo. This meant that she carried the whip, making sure that bitches followed Manolo's orders so that he stayed happy, and making sure no bitch tried to take her place.

"Oh, please believe, you still working today. I'm just not going to send you any clients. I need you to run to the store and grab some condoms and douches for me."

"No problem," Halleigh said as she smiled at the thought of a day off. She then hung up the phone and went over to finish her coke before leaving for the store, glad to play the role of errand girl over whore any day.

Scratch, the neighborhood crackhead, sat in the alley next to the store as his body yearned for another fix. He had been without a shot since earlier that day, and now here it was nighttime and it was like he was turning into a werewolf. His body throbbed as he clenched his stomach tightly. He frantically scratched his arms that felt itchy and irritated as if something was trying to burst up out of his skin. He stood up, trying to think of how he could get some money for his next fix.

Scratch walked out of the alley where the streetlights illuminated the sidewalk. In Scratch's 41 years, he had been through hell and back. He once was Flint's "push man," but now he was nothing more than a junkie. In the late eighties, he tried a dose of his own supply, and ever since then, he had been on the opposite side of the game, hooked on heroin and crack cocaine.

Scratch stood in front of the store pacing back and fourth, desperately seeking a way to get right.

"Ay, brotha. Look out for Scratch. Spare me a dollar, youngblood," he begged to a man walking out of the store.

The man ignored him and proceeded to his car. A pain shot through Scratch's stomach as his body went through withdrawal. As he clenched his stomach, he saw a beautiful girl in high heels and a mini-skirt walking into the store.

"Ay, baby girl. Can you spare a dolla'? Come on, baby girl, hook Scratch up," he begged as she walked right past him.

The bell over top of the store's door rang as the girl entered the store without paying Scratch a bit of mind. Her head was low, and it wasn't as if she was trying to ignore him like the man before her had so blatantly done, it was just that she was so consumed in her own personal thoughts that she hadn't heard a word that Scratch had said.

Scratch watched through the store's glass door as the girl stood in line at the counter, dug into her bra and pulled out wrinkled bills. His mind began to work overtime.

"Bingo!" Scratched whispered. He now had a plan.

Chapter Three

Halleigh had just walked down the street and into the corner store, still high from the line she had inhaled minutes before. She kept her head down, high as a kite as she picked up a few items and then stood in line.

As she had aimlessly strolled to the store, her thoughts suddenly landed on Malek somehow. Now she stood in the line, still consumed by thoughts of her former boyfriend, who she thought was going to be her future.

I miss that boy so much. I wonder if he ever thinks about me, she thought to herself. Halleigh's eyes watered as Malek's mother's words filled her head. *"Halleigh, I'm sorry to be the one to break this to you, but Malek left this morning. His father came into town and thought that it would be good for him if he got away from all this madness until things could die down and get cleared up. He didn't want to see you, honey."*

Halleigh caught a tear that had managed to escape her eye and wiped it away. She couldn't believe Malek had just upped and left her just like that. Her mind understood the words Mrs. Johnson had spoken, but her heart just couldn't believe them. Ironically, Mrs. Johnson couldn't believe she was telling Halleigh that bold face lie either. But she had to do something to keep Halleigh, who she always felt was no good for her son, away from Malek.

So after filling Halleigh's head with all those lies about Malek abandoning her and not wanting to see her, Mrs. Johnson had simply repented, making the excuse to God that she had done it for the sake of her son.

Lost in her thoughts, Halleigh didn't even notice the crackhead outside of the store that had been eyeballing her through the glass door. In all actuality, she never even noticed him when he tried to bum money from her before she ever even entered the store. But he had definitely noticed her.

Scratch searched frantically for a weapon in the alley so that he could try to rob the girl he had been scoping out inside the store. He felt bad about what he was about to do, but he had to get the monkey off of his back and quick. He grabbed a stick off the ground and quickly put it under his shirt, arranging it so that it stuck out, appearing to be a gun.

He leaned against the side of the building in the alley and awaited his prey.

"Give me yo' mu'fuckin' money!" Scratch whispered, trying to practice his approach. He looked down at the stick and knew that it wouldn't pass as a gun. "Damn!" he spat. "This shit ain't gon' work." He threw the stick down in frustration and became agitated as he sough out another weapon in the litter-filled alley.

Scratch knew that the girl would be walking out of the store any minute. He had to think quickly. He took off his worn-out shoe and then pulled off his soiled, stinky sock. He then gathered up a bunch of rocks that were on the ground and filled the sock. He held the sock up and the most horrendous odor reeked off of it.

"Well, goddamn!" he grimaced as the foul odor invaded his nose. "Whew! If the rocks won't knock her out, the smell sho' in the hell will," he said as he quickly removed the sock from his face.

Once again, Scratch leaned up against the wall and practiced his approach, which seemed even less threatening with a sock. "Fuck!" He knew that the "sock and rock" method wouldn't scare anybody and decided to go along with the fake gun approach.

He shuffled around real quick and found the stick that he had earlier discarded. But that's when he noticed a bigger one. He threw down the smaller one and took the bigger stick and placed it underneath his shirt as if he had a burner.

At that moment he heard the store's door bells

jingle, signaling, and then he heard the clicking of what he knew was the girl's high heel shoes. Just as he had anticipated, the girl came strutting out with a bag in her hand. He quickly ducked and leaned into the alley and waited for her to pass so he could grab her. His guilty conscious began to set in however. And in just those few seconds while he waited for her to cross his path, he went back and fourth with himself about going through with his plan. The little, red devil with the pitchfork sitting on his left shoulder got the best of him and when he saw the girl walk past him, he went for it.

He quickly grabbed her from the back and placed his hands over her mouth, dragging her into the alley and then slamming her against the wall. "Give me all yo' money!" Scratch demanded. He was shaking just as much as the girl was.

"Please don't hurt me!" she screamed, dropping the contents that were in her hands.

Scratch pushed her against the wall and pointed his fake gun at her. "Give me yo' cash and you won't get hurt," he whispered harshly.

"Please, don't kill me," she said, putting both of her hands up while her knees shook uncontrollably.

"Just give me all the dough and I won't shoot," Scratch assured her.

Just as Scratch had seen the girl do before, she anxiously went into her bra to pull out all the money she had. Scratch looked into the young girl's eyes and thought that she looked familiar. As he stared into her eyes, a frown quickly dropped.

"Halleigh?" he whispered as he lowered his fake gun.

She nodded her head. She was afraid to say anything. She didn't want to give him a reason to pop off.

"You Sharina's daughter, ain't you?" Scratch asked. He knew Halleigh's face well, because of Sharina; the two looked more like sisters than mother and daughter. Scratch knew that since it wasn't Sharina, it had to be her baby girl.

Sharina was one of Scratch's get-high buddies and he had seen pictures of Halleigh over at Sharina's house whenever he was over there getting high. He had even seen Halleigh in person a couple of times as well, but of course Halleigh never paid her mother's dope partners any mind.

Halleigh nodded her head and a small glimmer of hope ran through her. Since he knew her mother, maybe he really wouldn't hurt her. "Can you let me go?" she asked with her back still pressed against the wall.

Scratch looked down and forgot about the fake gun. "Oh yeah," he said as he dropped the stick, letting it fall onto the ground.

"You out here robbing people with sticks?" Halleigh said as a sense of relief passed through her body. She couldn't help but chuckle, although what she really wanted to do was take that stick and crack him upside the head for stupidity.

"It almost worked, didn't it?" Scratched replied, letting out a slight chuckle as well. "What is a girl like you doing out here on these mean streets this time of night, anyway?"

The last thing Halleigh wanted to do was stand out there and have a conversation with a man who had just robbed her. She wanted to leave the raggedy man in the alley, but she knew he had a Jones. She could tell, because she had seen the same look in her mother's eyes many of nights. And with that, thoughts of her mother and this man's relationship piqued her curiosity.

"I was just running to the store," Halleigh told the man and then quickly changed the subject. "How do you know my mother?" Halleigh replied.

"Me and Sharina used to get high together. How's she doing these days?"

"I don't know. I don't fuck with her like that no more."

"Well, hook me up, Lil' Rina . . . let me hold something so I can get right," Scratch begged her.

Halleigh was about to walk away and leave him there, but the fact that he knew her mother hit a soft spot with her. The fact that she had witnessed firsthand what a person was willing to do for a hit scared her. Yeah, he had spared her, but what about the next person? Before she handed him the money she asked, "What do you get from getting high off of crack? I never understood why my mother did it." Halleigh never even considered that cocaine really wasn't any better than crack. But Halleigh didn't see herself as being anything like the dope fiends she'd encountered who needed to get high. She just wanted to.

"So much fucked up shit has happened to me in my life, Lil' Rina. It's like when you're high all that goes away," he replied.

Halleigh peeled a twenty dollar bill from her stack of money and handed it to Scratch. She then began to walk away. Suddenly she stopped in her tracks and turned around and asked, "What did you say your name was?"

Scratch's eyes had lit up as he gazed at the money, knowing that he could finally get the monkey off of his back. He looked up at Halleigh with a gap-toothed smile and replied, "Scratch. E'vrybody know me as Scratch."

"Well, Scratch, don't get yourself killed out here robbing people with sticks," Halleigh said with a slight grin.

"You betta count yo' blessings, baby girl. I was going to unleash my stanking-ass sock on you with the ol' sock and rock," Scratch said jokingly, looking down at his one bare foot that he hadn't had time to put his sock and shoe back on.

Halleigh grinned and walked back toward the hotel.

"If you ever need to talk, come and holla at me. Good ol' Scratch! The rest of me might not be right, but I got good ears for listening. I'll be right here," Scratch yelled as he watched Halleigh walk away and into the darkness.

Coming Soon in 2009

A Pimp's Life

Prologue

My moms died today. The monster finally devoured her spirit and life. Sick the whole time through, she lived HIV-positive for fifteen years before finally succumbing to full-blown AIDS.

Drugs fucked up her whole shit up years ago. Fucked my whole shit up too. I watched her get high every day. It used to make me cry to see her after she hit that pipe. She'd be so lost in space. It was like her soul wasn't there, but her body was always there for anyone that could keep her high. I guess she finally reached that mountaintop she'd been climbing for so long.

What sense did it make though, when all she did was fall off? Maybe my father could've given her a helping hand. If she knew who that was. She'd had a child with a man from Virginia three years before I was born. She never knew what it was, and didn't want to know, putting up the baby for adoption the instant it was born.

I may as well have been adopted too because I didn't like the idea of admitting that my moms was a crackhead ho. She didn't love me. All she ever loved was that pipe. You know how that shit makes me feel? It don't make me feel like nothing. Because if you ain't never known love, then you ain't going to miss love.

Chapter One
MACK

I shielded my eyes from the glare of the afternoon sun as I walked out of Queens Courthouse. It had been a long night. I'd just spent it serving nine hours behind bars, thanks to the brave and dedicated hard work of New York City's Finest. I walked down the long row of cement steps and stood at the curb. The traffic lights were out, and cars headed east and west uncompromisingly whizzed by with no regard for pedestrians trying to make a dash for the island that divided the flow of traffic. I stood under the Don't Walk sign and pressed the button to no avail.

"Fuck it," I said, running into the street as soon as I saw a momentary clearing. I jumped on top of the divider and looked to my immediate right. Cars raced up the street as if this was the "Ghetto 500." My heart pounded through my chest from running, and my adrenaline rushed like Russell's when he was up in that elevator catching the full force of a J.B. beat-down.

Soon as I hit the sidewalk my cell rang. "Yo," I said, panting heavily, searching for air.

"You get out yet, jailbird?" Sade laughed.

Sade was my woman. We lived together in a house in Queens Village. She wasn't the best-looking woman I'd dealt with, but she had a good heart. Sade was 5-6, and was dark-skinned with full lips like Fantasia. Originally from Virginia, she'd moved to New York three years ago after her stepfather, Glen, tried to rape her. When she brought the issue to her mom's attention, her mom flipped the script by accusing her of lying and trying to cause a rift in her stable relationship.

When Sade's moms finally did confront Glen with the charges, he denied it, swearing up and down every crack of ass he'd ever licked that Sade came on to him. Deep in her heart, she knew she was wrong, so she let her daughter go and moved right along. She knew Sade was telling the truth and that he'd always had his eyes on her. I mean, why not? Here you had this young woman physically blossoming right before your eyes versus a sickly, one-tittie lady, slowly but surely withering away.

Afraid of spending the latter years of her life home alone, she chose his side, with her head down to the floor. That still bothered Sade to this day. She didn't understand how you could love somebody your entire life then just turn your back on them. None of the men her mother dated had good intentions.

Sade's moms was dying of breast cancer and had a huge life insurance policy. Every eligible bachelor in Richmond knew that she was worth four hundred thousand dollars after her ass expired. All she wanted to do was never die alone.

Sade would call her every now and again, but Glen always answered the phone and hung up when he heard her voice. Eventually he had the number changed, and Sade lost contact with her and refused to go visit her as long he was still living there.

"Yeah. I'm free. About to grab me some New York Fried Chicken from the Habeebs." I walked inside the restaurant. "Call Anton and tell him I said to come and get me. It's his fault I was in there in the first place," I said, sitting down. "Yo, Ahmed, let me get two thighs, small fries, and a lemon Mystic Iced Tea, man," I said to the owner. "Yeah, so, baby, did you miss me?"

"You know I did."

"Uh-huh. You better had."

"Whatever, Mack. I'm about to see the Dominicans. My hair needs to be washed and wrapped."

"Don't be out there spending up a whole lot of money, Sade. You heard?"

"Love you," she said, disconnecting the call.

I walked inside my Queens Village home and flopped down on the blue leather couch. I had been up the entire night madder than a mutha-fucka, sitting up in jail on some bullshit marijuana charge. I don't even smoke. My dude Anton was blowing one of them thangs down while we was in-side Cambria Heights Park with these two bitches. I don't know which was faster, the detectives that rolled up in the park in the black Expedition with tinted windows, or Anton's warrant-having ass hopping over the five-foot gate at the end of the park. He dropped the cigar shit right in front of me. So guess who it belonged to, according to the law? They let the girls off with a warning and let me ride in back of the truck with them.

The doorbell rang just as I'd reached my com-fort zone level. I ignored it at first, but the person continued to pound the fucking bell out. I looked through the peephole. "Ay, yo, who the fuck is it?"

Anton's big-ass head was all up in my view. I'm looking out the hole, his silly, non-complex ass is trying to look in.

"Open the door, man. You know I got warrants." He looked around before quickly rushing inside. Then he held out his hand. "Hey, man, apologies for last night."

"You's an ill dude, yo. I ain't fucking with you no more outside. I don't like being locked up. You just bounced without saying a word."

"If there was time to say anything, I would of. Look, I can't afford to get caught by these pigs, yo. They'll kill me. That's what they do when you shoot one of theirs."

I walked to the refrigerator, pulled two Heinekens from the top shelf, and popped the caps. "Whatever, man. Did you ever speak to them girls in Brooklyn . . . Kim's people?"

"Aw, man, I was caught up in some next shit, son. But I'm-a get up with her tonight and shit. Matter of fact, you should come too. She keep asking about you."

"Naw. I'm chilling at home with Sade. I didn't get to give her no 'daddy good loving' last night because of your ass." I pointed at him.

Anton took a long swig of the beer. "Gordy was asking about you too."

"Yeah? I don't hear my phone ringing off the hook. He ain't looking for me. He looking for something about me."

"Well, whatever the fuck"—He held out his hand—"I'm about to be out. Just came to check in on you and make sure you wasn't violated in the shower." Anton laughed.

"Fuck you!" I laughed. "Get the hell out my house," I said, pushing him out and closing the door.

Chapter Two

MACK

"I'm thinking about taking a trip to see my mother." Sade sat up in the bed. She leaned her back against the headboard and touched my chest. "You heard me, baby?"

"Naw. What's up?" I said, my eyes still closed.

"I said I want to see my mother. What do you think about that?"

"Sade," I said, sitting up, "if you want to see your mother, I'll roll with you down there. It's nothing."

"No, I need to do this by myself. I'll be all right."

"What about ol' boy?"

"I'll worry about that when I get there."

"You sure?"

"I'm a big girl, baby. I'll be cool."

"A'ight. I know you can handle yourself. So when you leaving?"

"I'm driving down there next Friday. I'll be gone for about three days."

I kissed her cheek.

"What was that for?"

"For being a real thorough bitch. That's the shit right there that made me fall in love with you."

Sade reached her hand under the covers and placed it on my hardening dick, massaging the head with her thumb. "And that's the shit that made me fall in love with you," she said, removing the covers from over me. She pulled my boxers off and slowly slid her mouth around the head of my dick and sucked it like a swollen thumb, licking around the rim and poking at the eye with the tip of her tongue.

I lay on my back looking at her, as she widened her mouth and long-throated the nine inches of "bless you with my loving." She gagged once, she gagged twice, but maintained the sexual discipline required to control tossing it up. When my body shivered, she sucked even harder.

"AWWWW SHIIIIT," I yelled out. "SADE. Oh my damn," I cried out as she continued milking the cow.

"What's the matter, boo? You can't take it?" she asked, my love fluids leaking from the corners of her mouth. "Where the freak at, daddy?" She rolled her tongue around at me then stuck it down my throat.

I lifted off her shirt and sucked on her hard, erect nipples, my mouth cruising around, on, and between her firm titties. I licked from her neck down to her navel and spoke to it in tongues. I melted down in between her legs and sniffed my pussy. And craved my pussy. I watched it as it throbbed and leaked in anticipation of a forthcoming tsunami.

"Come on, daddy, I wanna see lakes running down these sheets," she said, rubbing them with one hand while the other was snug behind my head.

I made her butterfly wings flap and her cat sing for tender victuals. I eloquently ran my tongue around the edges of each wing then quickly slid it further down. I pushed it up into her ass, and she sighed loudly. I razzled her and dazzled her with *tongue*nastic flips and twists, and turns and churns.

And then she farted in my fucking face. I was done.

"What happened, daddy?" Sade rubbed between her legs.

"Come on, man, how many times you going to fart in my face?"

She laughed. "Did it stink?"

"Oh, you think that shit is funny now, huh?" I playfully grabbed her by the shoulders and lay back down. "Come on, ma, get on top." I was standing strong as ever.

Wetter than a Mexican being rescued by the Coast Guard, Sade sat on it, and it slid straight up inside of her, the soft walls collapsing around me then constricting. As I lay still for a moment and let it burn, my body ushered in an even harder erection.

She planted her palms on my chest and slowly began to gyrate her hips a lil' something. She heard my black snake moan and matched it with a pleasurable meow. She leaned forward and grabbed my shoulders then began popping that thing up and down like hydraulics.

As we stared and growled at each other with the ferocity of a tiger and tigress, I grabbed her around the hips to secure her in place.

Sade threw her free hand in the air and slapped her own ass then froze, dragging her nails across my chest. "Baby, I'm about to cum." She grabbed my wrists. "Baby, I'm about to c-c-cum," she said, bracing herself this time. "HERE IT CUUMMSS," she yelled, happily rolling off me then laying absolutely still.

"Now that shit right there, baby"—I kissed her lips—"that shit right there was the best sex we ever had."

"Y-y-yeah," she responded, still a little shaken. "Maybe you need to spend the night in jail a little more often," she joked.

"That ain't funny," I said in all seriousness.

"Oh, you just need to stop it, Mack." Sade kissed my deflating showstopper. "Oh, what's going on here?" She lifted up ol' flappy. "Why you look so down?" She smiled at it. "You want mommy to make you happy again?"

I shook its head yes, and she went on ahead and made that fallen soldier a master sergeant.

Chapter Three

MACK

I was filling my gas-guzzling black Suburban up with some super unleaded at a Gulf gas station in Elmont, Long Island, and Anton was in my passenger seat, smoking a Philly and bopping his head to one of R. Kelly's cheaters-only anthems.

"I should take this shit to the carwash." I ran my finger across the door. "Every time it rains, I gotta get this shit washed." A horn beeped from behind my truck. I paid no attention to it, until it beeped again.

Anton looked out his window toward the back of the truck. "Be easy," he yelled out. "We almost done."

The horn beeped again, and I walked over to the green Infiniti, ready to knock somebody out. Pineapple-scented fresheners inside the car released a fragrance that clawed at the air when the window rolled down.

I'm a, I'm a, I'm a flirt
Soon as I see her walk up in the club, I'm a flirt

It had Virginia license plates and a decent-sounding stereo. The woman behind the wood-grain looked so good, I almost forgot why I walked over there in the first place. She was brown-skinned with chinky eyes and high cheekbones. Her lips were thin and coated with earth-toned gloss. She wore her hair cut short but straight, a couple of spikes toward the side of her head.

She turned her music down. "Well, what you want, playa?"

Winkin' eyes at me when I roll up on them dubs I'm a flirt
Sometimes when I'm with my chick on the low, I'm a flirt

"Why you keep beeping that horn behind us? You see how big that truck is? It takes a minute to fill up, you know."

"I got an appointment to get to. Traffic is going to be straight bananas on the Cross Island." She looked over at the traffic under the crosswalk.

"You'll make it. My shit should just about be filled."

I walked to the pump and pulled the hose out my gas tank. "You could've said the shit was fin-ished," I said, looking at Anton as I activated the auto-start. I pulled over some then walked back to her after she got out to pump her gas. "Hey, I'm sorry about that earlier." I extended my hand. "I thought you was some dick trying to be a smart ass. My name's Mack."

"No, it was just li'l ol' me." She smiled and bent over to pick up the gas card she'd dropped.

And when she's wit' her man looking at me, damn right, I'm a flirt
So, homie, don't bring your girl to me to meet, 'cause I'm a flirt
And, baby, don't bring your girlfriend to eat, 'cause I'm a flirt

Looking at her in the car, it was hard tell to that her legs were so thick, but she was firm and muscular, like really stacking, *mayne.* "So what's your name, love?" I looked down at my watch. I'd almost forgotten that we had somewhere to be too.

"Joi," she said, keeping an eye on the price of the gas tank. She placed the nozzle back in the holder and stood in front of me, her arms folded.

"Anyway, I do promotions at Club Phenomenon, down Rockaway Boulevard. I thought maybe one day you and some of your girlfriends could come through and show some love. We could always use a new face up in there, a fresh, fine face such as yours. First few drinks on me."

She looked at me and laughed. She put the hand down on the hood of her car to support herself from falling over. "You is mad corny, yo. Is that your best line?"

"Naw. My best lines come in li'l baggies about this size." I demonstrated with my fingers.

"Yeah? Well, I'm good on that. What you tryin'-a holla for anyway? You all cute in the face and what-not, I know you got wifey at home biting her nails down to the cuticle."

"Not even. I won't front though. I do have a lot of friends."

"Friends, huh? So I guess you just want me to be one of your new friends? Homie, lover, friend, fuck buddy?"

Please believe it unless your game is tight and you trust her
Then don't bring her 'round me 'cause I'm a flirt

"Yo, that's not even how I'm coming at you. Them other niggaz got your mind wrong. I just saw a pretty lady and took a chance. Besides, you never know when you may need a friend like me."

"Oh really? Let me ask you something? Do it look like I might be needing a friend's help any-time soon?" Joi chuckled. "Oh, you thought be-cause I'm from VA your New York accent was going to give you some sort of leeway into some drawers? I don't have time for this. I'm out." She opened her car door.

I totally ignored the bullshit Joi was spitting. "You got a man, Joi?"

"Something like that."

"A'ight. So let's cut the small talk. Here goes a

flyer and my card. Come on down and have a good time, baby. Promise, you won't regret it." I smiled.

Joi looked at me over her shades for a second then reached down into the cup holder inside her car. "You can call me after seven p.m. during the week. That's when my minutes start." She laughed.

"I hear ya, baby. So that's what's up. I'm-a holla at you real soon."

She stepped inside her car, beeping as she pulled off toward the Cross Island Parkway. Getting inside the truck, I said to Anton, "Now that's how you recruit, boy."

"Anybody could've done that. All you did was give the bitch a flyer. So what that mean? You keep talking about this pimping shit, but I ain't seen shit yet. You be fucking the strippers for free and all, but you not pimping."

"You'll see. Look at me, I am a gorgeous mutha-fucka, and women love that. Don't ever let no bitch tell you that looks don't matter. This is where it's at." I stroked my goatee. "This fly shit right here." I smiled, looking in my rearview, and pushed back my bushy eyebrows. "Personality is for psychologists," I said as I headed down Linden Boulevard.

A white-and-blue Q4 bus stopped at a red light in front of us and released a cloud of smog. "Close the windows," I said, turning on the vent. "This is why I hate coming down this block. I'm taking the back street." I turned left on 227th.

"So what you and Cocaine was talking about?"

"I'll let you know. Don't be opening your mouth about it either when we get to his house. You know how that nigga be getting when dudes start asking about shit he didn't bring up to them himself."

"I ain't worried about his ass. He might've put OPT together, but I'm the cat that be putting in all the work."

Cocaine, founder of OPT, On Point Killers, had more schemes, scams, and smarts than any man I ever knew. OPT was a team of thorough wolves based solely in New York City, known for getting that paper, and stomping in a head or two, if it came down to it. Non-believers became victims of the human pool table effect, eight balls in the corner pockets of our younger shorties-in-training hugging the block as if it were a surrogate father.

Cocaine was forty-six and straight out of an old school called "hard knock life." He was sentenced to ten years in prison when he was sixteen for killing Watty, his mother's boyfriend. Watty was beating the shit out of his mother one night and knocked her through a glass coffee table. Cocaine shot him with a gun he was holding for a friend. According to Cocaine, his mother only respected Watty when he was applying that chokehold around her scrawny little neck. And she only seemed to follow orders when she got a slap across the lips.

Even though it was some fucked-up shit to grow up seeing, it opened son's eyes in understanding a bitch. They wanted a man to be in control, to tell them what to do, and even welcomed a beating, minor or major, if they consciously ever stepped out of line.

All throughout Cocaine's entire life, he ain't

never saw any man love his mother. She never asked for respect. She was a poor excuse and a walking embarrassment in his eyes because, after it was really all said and done, it turned out his moms was a prostitute and a dope fiend. It was still etched in his head, the day he came home from school and his moms was fucking and doing dope right on his bed. Now if his own momma wasn't shit and he never felt what it was like to know that kind of love, how in the fuck could anybody ever expect that man to love and respect another woman?

Me and Cocaine met when I did two years of fed time for gun-running. We spent the last two years of his bid exchanging ideas. We got along so good that when I came home he had a spot for me in Queens Village and a lil' Honda Civic at the time. When I was put down with OPT, everything changed.

Cocaine had a stable of bitches working for him, regular bitches with jobs, others just trying to make a dollar. My job was to recruit for him. His clients consisted of average niggaz, white boys from Long Island and the Upper East Side of Manhattan, police, and some anonymous rappers. His biggest clientele was the husbands tired of the same ol' sloppy, aged, wrinkled pussy they was getting after twenty years of marriage and who left their desperate housewives crying their eyes out at home.

A lot of dudes was jealous because I didn't have to go through the initiation process they did. I got in because he knew I could make that dough for him. And if one more of them faggots questioned why I didn't get beat in, they'd be dead.

Cocaine usually didn't have to say anything twice. He had a short fuse. And an even shorter one when it came to his woman, Cakes, an ex-stripper from Michigan that he scooped at a party. She was on the books too. After he'd showed her what kind of bank he was dealing with, she was on the first Greyhound running. She was the epitome of what a dime should look like, 5-9, slender, bronze complexion. Her name was tatted across her chest and was followed by "Cocaine's Property."

She was his main investment, but there was a problem. He beat on her so bad at times that she couldn't always look presentable enough to work. He didn't like no one in the family looking at her unless she was on duty. She was *his* woman.

"Yo!" I knocked on Cocaine's front door. I said to Anton as he got out my truck, "Leave that window cracked so that shit don't be like no oven when we leave." I rapped on the door again. "Yo!"

"Who it is? What it be like?" he said, answering the door in a Rahsaan Ali robe. "Pimping." He smiled. "What's happening, broth?" He widened the door so we could enter.

"You know me. I just be doing what it do," I responded, standing in the patio.

"What's up, Ton? You gonna come in, or you just gonna stand there like a fucking porch monkey?" Cocaine laughed. "Get your ass on in here." He looked up and down the street before closing the door. He said to Anton, "You get my new strippers for the club yet?"

"I'm still working on it. The girl ain't been home. What you want me to do?" Anton shrugged his shoulders.

"Yeah, you absolutely right. What the fuck he gonna do, Mack?" Cocaine shook his head as we walked into the living room. He walked over to the stereo. "Y'all niggaz want something to drink?"

"You got some Grey Goose?" Anton asked.

"Yeah." Cocaine searched for the remote to his stereo. "What you want, Pimping?"

Before I could answer, his phone rang at the same time he found the remote.

"Yeah," he answered. "Look, Trish, you have your ass here before eight tonight. That's it," he said and disconnected the call.

No sooner had he stuck it down in the pocket of his robe than it rang again. He looked down at the caller ID display and frowned. "Looky here, y'all, I gotta take this call upstairs. Make your own drinks. You know where they at." He pressed power on the remote then jogged up the stairs.

The front door unlocked, and in walked Cakes, her hands filled with shopping bags. She was absolutely fucking gorgeous, man. She closed the door with the heel of her foot. "What's good, y'all?" She placed her bags in front of a blue reclining lounge chair next to a four-foot potted bella palm tree, where an automatic sterling silver mini-sprinkler connected to the hose of the bar's sink hose sprayed a misty dew every ten minutes.

Cakes' long, sexy, lotioned ass shined and stretched outside of her poom-poom shorts as she strode across the green living room carpet and placed her bags at the bar. "What y'all doing here?" She looked specifically at me, while pouring herself a drink. "What's up, boo? You looking kind of snazzy today. Where you off to, a job interview?" she sarcastically asked.

"Naw. I'm off to see the 'wizard' about some muthafucking brains, bitch." I grabbed my crotch like Michael Jackson after his acquittal.

Cakes chuckled. "That was actually funny. Anton, you all sitting up there like you don't acknowledge perfection in your presence, nigga. Hail a prominent ho when you see one, nigga." She bounced her ass off his leg.

"Hail the ho, hail the ho." Anton bent over laughing.

"That's right. My shit is magic on the johnson." She winked at me.

"So what you got over there?" Anton joked. "A bag of tricks?"

"Shit you can't afford on the salary you making."

Anton pulled out a roll of hundreds. "My pockets is fine."

"Pennies, nigga. You ain't getting it like Mack. Ain't that right?" Cakes smiled and looked at me.

"I'm not even in this. Y'all two always going at it. Shit, if I didn't know y'all wasn't stupid, I'd think you two was fucking."

"Yeah, me too," Cocaine said, stepping down

the last stair and into the end of the conversation. "But I know that ain't the case, right, y'all? Because there's a rule about fucking the help." He snatched Cakes' bags off the floor and threw them on the couch.

"Hi, daddy. I missed you." Cakes kissed his lips.

Cocaine turned his head and pushed her away. "You must be out of your mind, girl. What, you planning on going out on a date somewhere? What the fuck is all this bullshit, Cakes?" Then he started tossing shit out the bags onto the floor.

"I told you I was going shopping earlier. I can't be wearing repeat outfits when the work come in. I'm not like them other raggedy bitches you got munching and punching the clock, daddy. You know my style—Gots to look good for the customers."

As Cakes bent over to collect the fallen luxury items, Cocaine kicked her square in the ass. I could've sworn I saw a pound of that lotion on her shiny legs jump off her skin. She fell onto the pile of clothing in front of her and quickly turned over. Cocaine never liked anyone talking slick, especially no high-priced, hooker-ass ho. Especially when he was feeding and clothing them.

A tear rushed down her eye. "What the hell is you doing?"

"Get this damn shit off my living room floor, Cakes. You spent all of your allowance money on this bullshit. Get the fuck up to your room. NOW!"

Cakes quickly scrambled to her feet and stuffed

all the clothing back into the bags. Then she slowly walked up the stairs, rubbing her ass.

Anton and me looked at each other then looked at him.

"What?" Cocaine asked in a tone similar to Raphael Saadiq. "When the day comes I let one of my hoes talk to me like that, it'll be a rainy day in Southern California, you hear that? You give 'em one inch and they'll have you living in your own yard under the fucking gas meter." He sipped his drink. "Y'all muthafuckas know what I'm saying to you? Mack, you the next nigga up. I hope you paying attention. I'm trying to train your ass. You got potential, boy. Don't go letting me down."

Cocaine poured two shots of tequila, one for Anton, one for me. "Y'all niggas, have a drink with me." He held up his glass.

Anton told him, "You hard on these hoes, man."

"What, nigga? You need to be following in this man's footsteps." Cocaine pointed to me. "This fool is a pussy magnet. He bring the bitches into work."

Anton was upset. "And I don't?"

"You couldn't bring in the New Year without tripping over last month." Cocaine laughed. "You used to be on point. You slipping."

"What you mean, man? How much money and bitches I brought in last year?"

"That's not the point. It's all about chutes and ladders, baby."

Every now and again, when Cocaine had a little drink in his system, he'd just start making up some mind-boggling-ass phrase then build on it. Sometimes it'd make perfect sense; other times it sounded just as crazy as Gnarls Barkley singing the movie soundtrack for *One Flew over the Cuckoo's Nest.*

Anton asked, "What you mean, *chutes and ladders?*"

"Chutes and ladders, nigga." Cocaine coughed after inhaling deeply. "Rewards and consequences. You always start out on a good path, collecting points, respect, street cred and shit like that—That be the ladders that help you climb to the top of this game. Then you got them chutes—bitch-ass niggas, snitches, and informants, haters. Shit of that nature is the chutes that'll land your ass in a world of consequences. The chutes is the shit that'll make you fall, and it won't have shit to do with autumn. The whole idea of this pimp shit is to keep climbing the ladder until all the muthafuckas under you look like ants. This pimp shit be about the constant climb. The trick is to never look down, especially if you afraid of heights, muthafucka, because it's just not about pimping these hoes, it's about pimping the system. You ever lose focus of that, and you'll just be part of some bitch's photographic memory." He released a cloud of London fog.

"So what you saying, man?"

"I'm saying I see your true colors shining through, Ton."

"Yo, y'all is bugging," I said. "I got shit to do, Coke. You straight with that paper." I stood up.

Lately Cocaine had been stressing Anton about his inability to make things happen as he used to. He'd been that way ever since Anton had popped these two auxiliary police officers in Flushing Meadows, Queens a couple of months back. I felt in my gut that Cocaine wanted Ton dead, because his mouth would leak if he ever was caught by the pigs for that murder.

"Yeah, youngblood. We be done. Y'all seen my brother around? I ain't heard from him in a couple of days."

"Naw, man, not me," I said. "I just got out."

He said to Ton, "You, nigga?"

"I ain't seen him in a couple of days."

"All right, whatever. Hit my phone later, Mack," Cocaine said as we walked out the door. "We need to talk."